"Where Is Grakker?"

The monster's eyes were the size of watermelons, his orange skin the texture of a newly plowed field, his oddly split nose like a tree trunk putting down four major roots.

"Where is Grakker?" he bellowed in a voice like thunder.

His breath rushed past us like a windstorm, and smelled as if he had just eaten the county landfill.

I think it would have been perfectly reasonable for me to fall over dead with fear at this point. However, I actually managed to reply. My exact words, if I remember correctly, were something like, "Uh-uh-uh-b-duh."

"I want Grakker!" roared the monster.

Books by Bruce Coville

Camp Haunted Hills:
How I Survived My Summer Vacation
Some of My Best Friends Are Monsters
The Dinosaur That Followed Me Home

Magic Shop Books:
Jennifer Murdley's Toad
Jeremy Thatcher, Dragon Hatcher
The Monster's Ring

My Teacher Books:
My Teacher Is an Alien
My Teacher Fried My Brains
My Teacher Glows in the Dark
My Teacher Flunked the Planet

Rod Allbright Alien Adventures:
Aliens Ate My Homework
I Left My Sneakers in Dimension X

Space Brat Books:
Space Brat
Space Brat 2: Blork's Evil Twin
Space Brat 3: The Wrath of Squat

The Dragonslayers
Goblins in the Castle
Monster of the Year

Available from MINSTREL Books

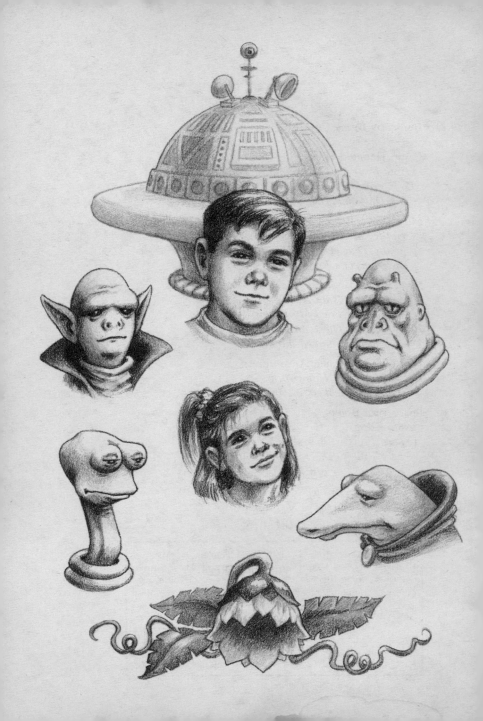

BRUCE COVILLE

I LEFT MY SNEAKERS IN DIMENSION X

Illustrated by Katherine Coville

A MINSTREL® BOOK

PUBLISHED BY POCKET BOOKS

New York   London   Toronto   Sydney   Tokyo   Singapore

A MINSTREL PAPERBACK *Original*

 A Minstrel Book published by
POCKET BOOKS, a division of Simon & Schuster Inc.
1230 Avenue of the Americas, New York, NY 10020

ISBN: 0-671-79833-2

First Minstrel Books paperback printing October 1994

10 9 8 7 6 5 4 3 2 1

A MINSTREL BOOK and colophon are registered trademarks of
Simon & Schuster Inc.

Cover art by Stephen Peringer

Printed in the U.S.A.

For Elise,
who keeps the boat afloat

CONTENTS

CHAPTER
1

Elspeth

WITH A CRY OF HORROR, I GRABBED MY THROAT AND began to gag. My face turned red. I staggered across the kitchen. After a moment I collapsed against a chair, staring at my mother.

"Tell me you're kidding," I gasped. "Tell me this is some horrible joke."

Mom was not amused.

"I am not kidding, Rod, and I don't want to hear any more about it," she replied in her special *I Really Mean It!* voice. "Your aunt Grace and uncle Roger are having some problems, and we are helping in the only way we can."

"Yeah," I moaned, sliding down so that I was flat on the floor. "By sacrificing *my* summer vacation."

Bonehead, my dog, came over and started licking my face.

"Having your cousin Elspeth stay with us for

a couple of weeks is not going to ruin your summer, Rod. It doesn't even have to ruin those two weeks."

"Are you kidding? You know what Elspeth is like."

My mother sighed. "I'll grant you that she's not the easiest child to get along with. But she *is* your cousin. And her parents really do need to get away."

"If Elspeth was my kid, I'd need to get away, too."

Mom didn't bother to answer. She didn't have to. The look on her face told me that it was time to shut up.

"I like Elspeth," said my sister, Little Thing One. (Her real name is Linda. But she's three years old, and at that age kids are very good at insisting on special names.)

"I like Elspeth, too," said her twin, Little Thing Two (also known as Eric, but mostly to my mother).

"You do not," I replied, sitting up. "The last time she was here she made you both cry, and you said you hated her."

"She won't make me cry this time," said Linda. "No one can make me cry anymore. Not since Grakker."

My mother rolled her eyes, but didn't say anything. I think that was because she had read some

2

book that told her it wasn't healthy to tell little kids that their imaginary friends weren't real. What Mom didn't know was that Grakker *was* real—as were Snout, Phil, Madame Pong, and Tar Gibbons, the other four little aliens that traveled through space with him on the good ship *Ferkel*. While I couldn't stop the Things from talking about the aliens, there was no way Mom was going to believe anything they said. This was just as well, since I was under strict orders from Grakker not to talk about the adventures that I had had with the aliens.

Mom turned her attention back to me. "Look, Rod, your cousin Elspeth is coming, and that's it. I want you to make her feel welcome. Is that clear?"

"Yes, ma'am," I said reluctantly. I try not to give her too much grief, since I know things have been hard on her ever since my father just took off shortly after the twins were born. Of course, things have been hard on me, too. But sometimes at night, when she thinks I'm sleeping, I hear her crying in her room. Those are the times when I think that if I could find my father, I would punch him in the nose. Except mostly I just want him to come home.

Anyway, even though I try to take it easy on Mom, I was not thrilled about having to spend the first two weeks of summer vacation with my bratty cousin Elspeth tagging around after me.

"It stinks," I said to my best friend, Mickey, the next morning, while we were waiting for the bus. "A kid waits all year for summer vacation, and then something like this has to happen."

"At least Billy Becker isn't pushing you around anymore," said Mickey, examining a grasshopper he had just caught.

He was right. Of course, what he didn't know was that Billy Becker wasn't exactly your run-of-the-mill sixth-grade bully but secretly a criminal mastermind from outer space. The reason he wasn't around anymore was that with my help Grakker and the rest of his crew had captured him. I wondered if Billy—or BKR*, as he was known in most of the galaxy—was still in the *Ferkel,* or if Grakker had actually delivered him to the place where he was to be held prisoner. Things had happened so fast when the aliens were around that I had never had a chance to ask a lot of the questions I had about how they traveled.

The bus came. Mickey put the grasshopper on my shoulder and climbed aboard. I flicked the bug away and climbed on after him. It was the

* Pronounced "Bee Kay Are"—editor

4

first day of the last week of school, and I was torn between two feelings. First was that delicious sensation that school was almost over, the happy anticipation of the vacation to come. Except in this case, that anticipation was tainted by my second feeling: dread at the arrival of my cousin Elspeth.

She wasn't even here yet and she was making me miserable!

That night I decided to take a look in my copy of *Secrets of the Mental Masters,* a book the alien named Snout had left me to study. So far it had not been as useful as I had hoped. The first chapter, for instance, consisted of two words: "Stay calm." I figured if this was what passed for secret knowledge in the rest of the galaxy, Earth wasn't as far behind the aliens as I had thought. On the other hand, when I considered how many people I had met who actually managed to follow that advice, I wondered if maybe there was more to it than I realized.

"Okay," I told myself. "I'll get calm. Knowing Elspeth, it won't be easy. But I'll do it."

Living in the same house as Thing One and Thing Two gave me lots of opportunities to practice staying calm under all sorts of circumstances. By the time I got through the birdseed in my underwear incident without exploding, I was feeling pretty confident about my calmness.

5

Then Elspeth arrived, and I realized I was going to need a whole library of alien advice to stay calm with this kid around.

"Hi, Roddie!" she exclaimed as her mother led her through the door. "No luck with the diet, huh?"

I began to blush. It's not like I'm fat or anything; just a little chunkier than I would like. I certainly didn't need Elspeth to remind me of it.

"He likes ice cream too much," said Little Thing One.

(That was another problem with Elspeth: She brought out the worst in the twins.)

"And chapato pips," added Little Thing Two.

"I like them, too. But I'm skinny anyway." He pulled up his shirt to prove the point.

"That's enough, Eric," said my mother.

It didn't take long for Aunt Grace to say her good-byes. After giving Elspeth a hug, she scurried out the door.

"Have a good time!" called my mother. This seemed unnecessary to me; now that she had dumped Elspeth with us, Aunt Grace's life was bound to improve.

It was *my* future that was looking bleak.

By the next day I was ready to imitate my father and run away from home. Elspeth's nonstop chatter—combined with her need to point out every flaw in my face, body, clothing, and room—was driving me berserk.

"I think I'll take Bonehead out to Seldom Seen for a while," I said to my mother, after breakfast.

Seldom Seen is what we call the field behind our house. We live out in the country, and our backyard slopes down to a swamp thick with big old willow trees. On the far side of the swamp, surrounded by woods, is a big field where Grampa still grows corn. He named it "Seldom Seen" because—well, because it's seldom seen. You can only get to it by crossing the swamp on a little wooden bridge my father and some of his friends built, or by going through a neighbor's automobile junkyard.

It is a very private place, and I love it out there. I had intended to go on my own. So you can imagine how pleased I was when my mother said, "That's a good idea, Rod. Why don't you take Elspeth along?"

I sighed. It wasn't even worth fighting about. I knew I would lose. At least she didn't make me take the twins. (This was just as well, considering what was waiting for me out there.)

I started to put on my new sneakers, which were sort of a bribe from Mom for putting up with Elspeth, and got ready to leave.

"Do you think you should wear those, Rod?" asked Mom—meaning, of course, that *she* didn't think I should wear them. They were expensive, and I knew she had had to stretch the budget to buy them. But what was the use of sneakers if you couldn't wear them? Even so, I might have changed my mind, if Elspeth hadn't chimed in.

"Your mother's right," she said primly. "You'll probably get them all muddy crossing the swamp."

I grunted and continued tying my laces. Mom sighed and turned away. I felt bad, but not bad enough to take off the sneakers.

With Elspeth bouncing along behind me, and Bonehead bouncing along behind her, I headed for the swamp.

I figured things couldn't get worse, until we actually made it to Seldom Seen and stumbled into a hole. It was enormous—about a foot deep and nearly twenty feet long. I knew it would upset my grandfather, because whatever had made it had mashed down the young corn stalks.

Then I realized what the hole really was. I stopped worrying about what my grandfather would think and concentrated on staying calm. It wasn't easy. My heart pounding with terror, I whispered, "Let's get out of here, Elspeth."

"Why? I like it back here."

"Don't you see what this is?" I asked.

She made a face. "Yeah, it's a hole in the ground. So what?"

8

I swallowed, then pointed to the front of the hole, yards away, where I could see four distinct marks.

Toe marks.

"This isn't just a *hole*," I hissed. "We're standing in a footprint!"

CHAPTER
2

Smorkus Flinders

ELSPETH BEGAN TO LAUGH. "YOU DON'T THINK I'M dumb enough to fall for that, do you?"

"Shhhh!" I hissed. Though she was talking in a normal tone of voice, to my terrified ears it sounded as loud as a scream. I figured anything that might attract whatever had made that footprint could be fatal.

Elspeth ignored my terror. "This is amazing," she said, starting to walk the length of the print, which had a series of puddles in the bottom of it. Bonehead had already raced from one end to the other, sniffing frantically.

"I'm impressed, Roddie," said Elspeth when she reached the far end. "It really does look like a footprint. You even gave it claw marks. How did you do this, anyway?"

"I didn't *do* it, Elspeth, it's real! Come on, let's get out of here while we can."

I grabbed her hand, intending to drag her away. "Stop it, Rod!" she shouted.

The jolt of fear that shuddered through me was something like the feeling I had had the time I was nearly hit by a car while trying to catch someone I mistakenly thought was my father.

"Don't shout," I pleaded, keeping my voice as low as I could. "Don't do *anything* to attract attention."

Her peal of laughter would have woken a stone. "I didn't know you could act, Rod! You're really good. Have you been in any plays at school? My mother says—"

Her chatter was interrupted by the arrival of the creature in whose footprint we were standing, at which point it became clear that my initial reaction of sheer, stark terror had been the correct one.

The monster came at us out of the woods, wading through the trees as if they were water. He was so tall—easily four times as tall as my house—that I wondered if he had been lying down until now. His eyes were the size of watermelons, his orange skin the texture of a newly plowed field, his oddly split nose like a tree trunk putting down four major roots. The ground shook when he walked, though it took him only three steps to reach us. Staring down at us, he said, "Where is Grakker?"

His voice was like thunder. His breath, which rushed past us like a windstorm, smelled as if he had just eaten the county landfill.

I think it would have been perfectly reasonable of me to fall over dead with fear at that point. However, I actually managed to reply. If I remember correctly, my exact words were something like, "Uh-uh-uh-b-duh."

"My name is Smorkus Flinders," roared the monster, "and I want *Grakker!*" Reaching down, he scooped me into his hand. His fingers were the size of small tree trunks, his skin as rough as a gravel driveway.

For good measure, he grabbed Elspeth with his other hand. She was screaming, which I couldn't blame her for, since I was doing the same thing. Don't get me wrong; I had faced enough scary moments during my adventures with Grakker and the gang that I think I can safely say I'm not a coward. But this was something else altogether. The creature holding us now would have been terrifying even if he was the nicest person in the universe—which I had no reason to believe he was. One squeeze and he could have popped me like a pimple; one bite and he could have removed my head as easily as you nip a grape from its stem. So I hope you'll excuse me for experiencing a level of terror unlike anything I had ever known before.

"Grakker! Grakker! Grakker!" said the monster, shaking me up and down like a baby's rattle.

I tried to answer, but my voice seemed to have gotten stuck somewhere inside my throat.

The monster raised his hand so that I was right in front of his face. His eyeball was bigger than my head.

"Where did Grakker go?"

"I don't know," I answered. At least, I tried to. My voice came out in a tiny squeak.

"I can't hear you!" he roared.

I wondered if he would get angry if I wet my pants, which was beginning to seem like a real possibility.

"I don't know!" I repeated.

I was louder this time, I'm sure. But obviously not loud enough.

"I still can't hear you!" he roared.

Then he stuck me in his ear.

This was, without a doubt, the most disgusting thing that had ever happened to me in my life. I was jammed into Smorkus Flinders's ear canal all the way to my waist. My arms were pinned to my sides. From the bits of light that leaked in around my body, I could see a boulder-size chunk of ear wax just inches from my face. Hairs the thickness of tree twigs sprouted all over its surface. On the hairs were swarms of tiny, aphid-like green bugs.

13

For a minute I was afraid the monster was going to shove me all the way in. Maybe that wasn't a reasonable fear. Considering the circumstances, I am not ashamed to say that I was feeling completely unreasonable.

"Talk louder!" roared my captor. "Where . . . is . . . *Grakker?*"

"I don't know!" I screamed.

At least he was able to hear me this time. "You must know," he said. "He was here, was he not?"

If I had any brains, I would have lied. But I had only learned to lie a little while ago, and I still wasn't very good at it. Besides, the way I was thinking at the moment, my brains might as well have been made of tapioca pudding.

So I told the truth. "Yes, he was here."

The monster made a growling sound deep in his throat. For a horrible second I was afraid he was going to shove me the rest of the way into his head and just leave me there. But after a moment he said, "Good. That is what I wanted to know." Then he pulled me out of his ear and transferred me to the hand that held Elspeth.

She was still screaming. I hoped the monster wouldn't get tired of listening to her and decide to just give us a little squeeze. We probably would have oozed out of his hand like toothpaste from a tube.

It's weird the stuff that runs through your

mind when you're in danger. Even as I was wondering if I was going to be alive thirty seconds from now, I was also hoping that if I never got home again my mother wouldn't think I had just run out on her.

I heard Bonehead barking in the distance. Looking down, I saw that he was nipping at the monster's heels. What a brave little dog! Fortunately, Smorkus Flinders didn't notice him. I couldn't have stood it if he had stepped on the little guy.

Our captor sniffed the air a few times, then turned back in the direction from which he had come. Then he did something even more frightening than picking us up, more frightening than sticking me in his ear, more frightening, in his case, than existing.

Using his free hand, *he tore a hole in the air.*

It was weird, as if the world was a giant movie screen, and he was ripping through it into somewhere else.

Beyond the hole was someplace dark and strange.

Growling like a thunderstorm, still clutching Elspeth and me in his rocky paw, the monster stepped through the hole.

I could hear Bonehead barking frantically behind us. Then the monster pulled the hole shut and everything was silent.

CHAPTER
3

Castle Chaos

I DON'T KNOW HOW TO DESCRIBE THE PLACE WE EN-tered, except to say that somehow it felt as if it was shaped wrong. Shifting forms, unconnected to anything, floated in the air. The sky looked like boiling purple water, the ground like a pot of overcooked macaroni. Only I don't think *ground* was the right word, since I suddenly realized that our captor was walking waist deep through— through whatever it was. The sight was so weird my stomach rolled over as if I were in a roller coaster that had just done a complete loop.

"Take us home!" bellowed Elspeth. "TAKE US HOME RIGHT NOW, YOU CREEP!"

My sentiments exactly. Not that Smorkus Flin-ders paid any attention. Of course, it was easy for him to ignore us; he probably couldn't hear us, even though we were screaming at the top of our lungs.

After a while it became clear that (1) he was not going to squish us right away and (2) he was not going to pay attention to a word we screamed. We stopped struggling, partly because it wasn't doing any good, partly because we were exhausted.

"Rod, what's happening?" whispered Elspeth.

The whispering was unnecessary, of course, given the fact that even if you were yelling this guy had to jam you into his ear before he could hear you. But Elspeth's tear-stained face was so frightened I decided not to point that out. So I just said, "I don't know."

"Who's this Grakker guy he wanted to know about?"

I hesitated for a second, then replied, "He's sort of an alien police officer."

Normally that would have gotten me a snort of disbelief. Under the circumstances, Elspeth didn't have much choice but to accept it.

"How did you meet him?" she asked.

Considering our situation, I couldn't see much point in secrecy. So I told her everything that had happened after the good ship *Ferkel* had crashed into my tub of papier-mâché earlier that spring.

Elspeth listened to the story with wide eyes. When I was done, she said, "That's amazing! But I still don't understand what it has to do with this guy."

"I don't have the slightest idea," I said, shaking my head. A huge shape, something like a cloud but thicker and red, went swimming (that's the only word that makes sense) past us. I shuddered, wondering if we had any chance at all of leaving this world alive.

I don't know how long we traveled, or how far we went. Given the size of the creature who had kidnapped us, it didn't take that many steps to go a mile. On the other hand, the world we had entered was so weird I wasn't sure it made sense to measure things in normal ways. More than once we walked through something that looked like a hole in the air—not the kind of opening the monster had ripped in the air to bring us here, but a huge floating oval that brought us out someplace altogether different from where we started.

The ground shifted and moved beneath us as we traveled; sometimes our captor was walking on it, sometimes through it.

We crossed a valley where multicolored streamers dangled from the sky, shooting off huge sparks whenever they happened to touch each other. In another place house-sized bubbles of mud drifted up from the ground, some bursting open to spatter in all directions, others floating off until they disappeared in the boiling purple sky.

Occasionally we saw other monstrous creatures shambling along in the distance. None of them came very close to us.

Eventually I saw a building somewhere ahead of us. Or at least *part* of a building. Some of it was visible, but the walls seemed to end in odd places, as if something had chopped off big chunks of it. It was hard to figure out the size of the building at first, because I had nothing to compare it to except the boiling purple sky. But as we drew closer, I began to sense that it was built on the same scale as our captor—which meant that it was unbelievably enormous.

It had no doors that I could see. This did not stop Smorkus Flinders. He simply walked through the wall.

The room we entered was like a cavern, the ceiling so high it was lost in distant darkness. We passed through two or three more such rooms, which did not seem to be connected in any way that made sense, until we found ourselves in a somewhat smaller room—meaning the ceiling was only a little way past our kidnapper's head.

A table, or something like a table, stood against one wall. On the table was a cage. Smorkus Flinders thrust his hand into the cage, dropped us to its floor, then withdrew his hand and closed the door. Putting his eyeball close to the cage, he looked at us for a moment. I thought about trying to punch him in the eye, but figured he would just squash me. Since I didn't want to end up as a grease spot on a table in another dimension, I held still. (The fact that I was too terrified to move probably had something to do with this as well.)

"Grakker will come for you," he said confidently in a voice like thunder. "Even here in Castle Chaos, he will come for you."

Then he turned and left the room, which he did by once again walking through a wall.

I wondered if the monster was right about Grakker. Though I was not happy about being used as bait to draw my alien friends into a trap, the idea that someone might actually try to rescue us was the only thing that kept me from dissolving in complete terror.

Elspeth didn't have that hope. When I turned to say something, I found her huddled in a corner of the cage, her arms around her knees, her head pressed against them so that I couldn't see her face.

I went and sat next to her.

"What *was* that thing?" she whispered after a moment.

"I don't have the slightest idea. But did you hear what he said? He expects Grakker to come and rescue us."

"When?" asked Elspeth dully.

For that question, I had no answer.

I stared at the walls of the gigantic room, wishing I had read more of Snout's book on the secrets of the mental masters when I had had the chance. "Stay calm" was probably a good starting place for getting out of this situation alive, but it certainly wouldn't do the job on its own.

I took a deep breath, counted to ten, and began to examine our prison. It was shaped something like a birdcage, with a rounded top and a door that went halfway up the wall. It had nearly as much floor space as my bedroom. The bars were thick as my wrists and spaced about four inches apart. I grabbed two of them to see if they would bend. That might sound stupid, but it would have been even stupider not to try. Their silky surface felt nice, but when I tried to shake them, they released a smell like rotten eggs.

Coughing, I let go and rubbed my hands on my pants.

The smell persisted.

I went back and sat beside Elspeth.

"What are my parents going to do?" she whispered.

I started to mouth off about how her parents had dumped her with us, but decided not to. The fact that Aunt Grace and Uncle Roger had wanted to get away from her for a few weeks didn't mean they wanted her gone for good. Besides, it got me thinking about my own mother. She already had to deal with the fact that my father had just picked up and disappeared about three years earlier. I was afraid my being missing was really going to break her heart.

"Grakker will come for us," I said. "You'll see."

I honestly don't know whether I was trying to convince Elspeth, or myself.

After a while, we both fell asleep. (You may wonder how we could sleep under the circumstances, but I'll tell you, terror can be exhausting.)

I was woken by someone entering the room.

It wasn't Grakker and the other aliens.

It wasn't Smorkus Flinders.

This was a new creature altogether, smaller but also uglier, which I would have thought was impossible.

"My, aren't you a juicy looking pair?" he said.

Drooling, he rubbed his hands together and began walking toward our cage.

Elspeth and I huddled against the bars as the new monster approached our cage. He was big, blue, and blubbery, with rolls of fat that wobbled as he walked. He had three squinty eyes—two in the regular places, one centered above them—

each topped by a thick brow. He was naked except for a large ring in his right ear, and something that looked pretty much like an orange diaper.

This is it! I thought in horror. *I lived through Billy Becker only to end up mashed between the molars of a big blue blob?*

The monster began fumbling with the door of the cage. Elspeth and I slid as far back as we could, huddling together and pressing ourselves against the bars as if we could push our flesh right through them. For a moment, I hoped Big Blue's pudgy fingers would be too clumsy to work the door.

No such luck. It sprang open.

He reached into the cage. We squirmed and tried to escape, but there was nowhere to run. In only a moment his fingers closed around us.

"Yummy!" he cried, pulling us from the cage and holding us in front of his face.

We continued to scream.

"Quiet, supper," he rumbled. Then he tipped back his head and lifted us over his mouth. A river of drool was running from the corner of it. Smiling, he opened wide.

I felt as if I was looking into a cavern. The monster's jagged green teeth were like stalactites and stalagmites, his gullet like a tunnel that led into a deeper, endless darkness.

He opened his hand. Still screaming, we clung to his fingers, dangling above the great blue pit of his mouth.

He gave his hand a shake. I gripped his fat finger even more tightly. My cousin was not so lucky. She lost her hold and tumbled into his waiting mouth.

He closed it, and smiled in satisfaction.

CHAPTER
4

Spar Kellis

A VARIETY OF THOUGHTS WERE COLLIDING IN MY mind. I was horrified for Elspeth, terrified that I would be next, and at the same time trying to figure out what I would tell my mother about Elspeth if I ever got out of this. I am not particularly proud of that last, but Snout has told me that we are not so much responsible for the things that rise from our minds as for what we do about them. Which was the other thing that I was thinking about: What to do.

The monster was close. If I let go of his finger and landed on his face, could I squiggle into his nose and make him sneeze?

If I did, would Elspeth come flying out of his mouth?

Would either of us survive the force of that kind of explosion?

Unable to come up with any other plan, I was

about to drop to his face, when a voice exploded from somewhere in the distance. "Spar Kellis, let go of those children!"

A guilty look crossed the huge blue face beneath me. Lifting his hand, Spar Kellis spit Elspeth into his palm.

She was very wet and bedraggled, but alive.

She was also upset. Looking up at where I still clung to Spar Kellis's other hand, she screamed, "I'm going to tell your mother, Rod!"

Pure Elspeth. Instead of being glad she was alive, she was looking for someone to get in trouble. I didn't let it upset me. For one thing, I doubt I could have been any more upset if I tried. For another thing, if we got out of this alive, I didn't care *what* she told my mother.

I think she was going to yell at Spar Kellis next. Before she could start, Smorkus Flinders loomed over his shoulder and said, "Put them back in the cage, you fool. I'm using them for bait!"

I could tell by the way he held his face that he was whispering, the way people do when they get really angry. The thing is, for this guy a whisper sounded something like a bomb blowing up.

Spar Kellis, who was about a head shorter than Smorkus Flinders, made a cranky face. But he did as he was told, thrusting first Elspeth and then me back into the cage.

Elspeth was trying, without much success, to wipe the monster slobber off her arms. "I hate you!" she hissed at me.

Like it was all my fault.

Outside the cage Smorkus Flinders had grabbed Spar Kellis by the ear and was bawling him out. Somehow this made me feel better.

"These two are to be kept alive and in fairly good condition until someone comes to rescue them," said Smorkus Flinders. "Besides, you know you're not supposed to eat anyone in this dwelling without my permission. Isn't that right?"

With that he squeezed the blue guy's ear, which caused him to squeal in what I assume was pain.

"Isn't that right, Spar Kellis?" repeated our kidnapper.

"Yes, oh Glorious One," whined the blue monster. "Of course. Absolutely. You couldn't be more correct if you tried."

With a snort Smorkus Flinders let go of Spar Kellis's ear. "As punishment for your presumption, it will be your job to keep these two alive and healthy until my trap is sprung. Is that clear?"

"Yes, Your Magnificence."

"Then see that it is done." He gave Spar Kellis a whack on the head that would have flattened a moose, then turned and left the room, which he did by walking through the ceiling. At least, that was what it looked like.

My ears felt like I had been stuck in a thunderstorm.

The blubbery blue monster sighed, which almost knocked me over. Bending down so that his three eyes were in front of the cage, he said, "You two got me in a lot of trouble."

"*We* got *you* in trouble?" I yelped. "You were going to eat us! Talk about trouble! Where would we have been then?"

"In my tummy," said the blue monster happily.

"I hate you," said Elspeth. "I hate both of you." Then she turned around and stared out of the back of the cage.

I figured that, like me, she felt safe now that Smorkus Flinders had made it clear Spar Kellis was not to harm us.

"I hate you, too," said the blue monster, making the kind of face a three-year-old might make under the circumstances.

"Don't mind her," I said. "She's always that way."

"Shut up, Rod," said Elspeth, without turning around.

I shrugged. "See what I mean?" I said to the monster.

I wasn't just talking for the sake of talking; I hoped if I could get Spar Kellis talking, too, I might be able to get some useful information out of him. If my ears could survive the conversation.

"I have a sister like that," he replied with a frown.

"This one is my cousin."

"Shut up, *Roddie*," repeated Elspeth.

Spar Kellis rolled his eyes. The effect was very strange, considering that he had three of them, all bigger than bowling balls. "Glad I'm not you," he said.

I shrugged again. "At the moment she's the least of my troubles."

Spar Kellis thought for a second, then nodded his huge blue head. "I see what you mean. You are in a pretty bad situation." He paused, then added, somewhat wistfully, "Really, it might have been better for you if I had just eaten you and gotten it over with."

That certainly didn't make me *feel* any better, let me tell you. In my head I repeated the motto of my favorite character, John Carter of Mars. (He starred in a whole bunch of books by the same guy who invented Tarzan.) No matter how bad things got, John Carter always said, "I still live!" His theory was that as long as he was alive, he had a chance to get out of whatever mess he was in.

I figured that was the best attitude to take in this situation.

Of course, John Carter's adventures were just stories. This was real life.

"After all, instant death wouldn't be much worse than being held captive by Smorkus Flinders," continued Spar Kellis. "Might even be better."

"Would you mind talking a little bit softer?" I shouted, putting my hands over my ears.

He looked puzzled, then blinked, as if he realized what I meant. "I always forget about the way my voice affects you small ones," he said.

"Small ones?" I asked, wondering if most of the people in this place were closer to my size than his.

Rather than answering, he wrinkled his blue face and said, "I don't think Smorkus Flinders wants me to talk about that."

"How come Smorkus Flinders gets to boss you around?"

Big Blue looked at me as if I had lost my mind. "Because he's bigger than I am," he said, as if that explained everything. "Besides, I work for him. It's not easy."

"I bet it's not," I said sympathetically. "So tell me, Spar Kellis—that is your name, isn't it? Spar Kellis?"

He gave me a goofy grin. "That's right!" he said, as if I was some kind of genius for figuring it out.

"So tell me, Spar Kellis: How come you speak our language?"

"Don't be silly! I don't speak your language. *You're* speaking *my* language."

I blinked, then blinked again as I realized that what he said was true. Now that I stopped to think about it, the words coming out of my mouth were not only not English; they didn't sound like *any* language I had ever heard.

What was going on here?

"Dimensional transfer side effect," said Spar Kellis, giving me a gap-toothed grin. "If you travel between dimensions the right way, it alters your brain so you can understand the beings on the other side. It's not easy, of course. I mean, any dimensional crossing is terribly difficult, and doing it this way is even harder. But Smorkus Flinders wouldn't do it any other way. He's sort of a perfectionist."

I put my fingers to my temples uneasily, wondering what else this little trip might have done to my brain.

"Tell me more about Smorkus Flinders," I said.

I noticed that Elspeth had turned around and was listening to the conversation.

Spar Kellis shuddered, which made his huge cheeks wobble. "My glorious boss is known across six dimensions for his cruelty."

I was surprised. "I thought cruelty was considered the greatest crime in the civilized galaxy," I said, remembering what Madame Pong had told me about BKR.

"*Your* galaxy, maybe," replied Spar Kellis. "But remember, you come from a different dimension."

"What dimension is this?"

"We call it Dimension X. It's sort of next door to yours, if you just vibrate a little differently. Not that changing the way you vibrate is that easy. . . ."

"Nothing I've ever been able to manage," I said.

Spar Kellis looked at me oddly, and I realized he didn't understand that I was joking. Maybe he just didn't have a sense of humor. Or maybe humor doesn't make transdimensional crossovers. It was hard to tell.

I decided it would be best to change the subject. "What does your 'glorious boss' want with us?" I asked.

Spar Kellis frowned. "I'm not sure. He said someone was going to try to rescue you. Do you know who?"

"Yeah. A guy named Grakker."

Spar Kellis's three eyes got even rounder and bigger than they were already. He took a step back from our cage. "Uh-oh," he said. "You really *are* in big trouble!"

CHAPTER
5

The Pandimensionality

THE MONSTER'S WORDS MADE MY STOMACH TIGHTEN. I heard Elspeth moan behind me. "What are you talking about?" I asked Spar Kellis nervously.

He rolled his two outer eyes toward the center. "My glorious boss *hates* Grakker for what he did to his best friend."

"Who is his best friend?" I asked, feeling even more nervous than before.

"A nasty little guy named BKR. He's the only person in your dimension as cruel as Smorkus Flinders. It made for a special friendship between the two of them. Grakker is BKR's archenemy, and not long ago he managed to arrest him for his crimes. Smorkus Flinders is out for revenge."

And what would Smorkus Flinders do if he found out that I had helped Grakker arrest BKR? I wondered nervously. *Maybe decide to skip using me for bait and just make me the object of his revenge instead?*

"Isn't that interesting?" I said, trying to keep my voice from trembling.

"What's your connection to Grakker?" asked Spar Kellis.

Now here was a tricky question. Even though I had finally gotten past my compulsive truthfulness and learned to lie when the occasion called for it, I didn't want to deny a friend. It seemed traitorous, somehow. On the other hand, given the situation, it was hard to tell just how dangerous the truth might be. ("Oh, you're actually a *friend* of Grakker's, eh? Sorry, but we're going to have to turn you into a jam sandwich!")

I can't say I was particularly quick in coming up with a skin-saving answer. But then, the weirdness of talking to someone whose face took up my entire field of vision did make thinking fast a little difficult.

Somewhat to my surprise, it was Elspeth who bailed me out. Breaking free of her sniveling mode, she walked to the front of our cage and said, "Grakker made Rod do something once. I don't know the guy at all. What's he like?"

Thanks, cousin, I thought. *I owe you one.*

Spar Kellis looked a little puzzled. "I don't know," he said. "I never met him myself. I just know my glorious boss wants his skin."

35

"Just who is your glorious boss?" asked Elspeth, wiping the tears from her cheeks with the back of her hands. "I mean, I know his name, but who is he? The king or something?"

Spar Kellis smiled proudly. "Smorkus Flinders is the most important creature in Dimension X."

"Why?" persisted Elspeth.

"Because he's the biggest."

"You judge people based on size?" I asked incredulously.

"Don't you?" replied the monster.

No sooner did I start to deny the idea than my rebellious brain began supplying examples of times when we did just that—starting with my own experiences on the playground of Cherry Street School. That was one of the problems in dealing with alien creatures; they constantly made me look at the way we did things with a fresh eye, and I often did not like what I saw.

While I was dithering over matters of size, Elspeth picked up our end of the conversation. "Tell me a little more about Dimension X," she said.

Spar Kellis paused. "Well, it's known as one of the five strangest dimensions in the Pandimensionality," he said at last.

"The *what?*" I asked.

"The Pandimensionality. It's sort of a collection of dimensions."

"Just what is a dimension, anyway?" asked Elspeth.

36

Spar Kellis wrinkled all three of his brows. "Well, it's sort of like a universe. Except when you start talking in terms of dimensions, it means you're aware that several universes can exist side by side."

"But isn't the universe supposed to be infinite?" asked Elspeth.

Spar Kellis shrugged his blubbery shoulders. "I guess so."

I saw what Elspeth was getting at. "But something that's infinite goes on forever," I said. "How can you have more than one infinitely big thing? Wouldn't they run into each other?"

"Of course not!" he snorted. "They vibrate differently, so they can be in the same place at the same time."

"So Dimension X and our dimension exist in the same place?" I asked.

"Where else could they be?" he replied, as if he couldn't believe I was asking such a dumb question.

"I'm not sure I understand," I said.

Spar Kellis did his eye-crossing trick. "I don't make the rules. I'm just trying to answer your questions—though now that I think of it, I probably shouldn't be doing that." Suddenly he narrowed his eyes, which made them sort of like squashed bowling balls. "Were you two trying to trick me?"

"Trick you into what?" asked Elspeth.

"Trouble!"

He shivered, and I got the sense that getting in trouble with his glorious boss was the most horrifying thing he could think of. Without another word he turned and left the room.

Unlike Smorkus Flinders, he did not go through the ceiling.

He went through the floor.

At least, that was what it looked like. But now that I actually looked at them, I suspected the walls were not where they had been the last time I checked, so maybe it wasn't the floor after all. This whole place seemed to shift when you weren't watching it. (If you think it's confusing to imagine, you ought to try living it!)

For a long time neither Elspeth nor I said anything. Not that we didn't have plenty to talk about. But we were both too exhausted to do much more than sit and stare at each other. After a while Elspeth crawled over to the side of the cage and curled up against it. She started to cry.

"Don't," I said.

"Why not?"

I didn't have any answer for that. Crying was perfectly reasonable under the circumstances. I just knew that usually when someone was crying you were supposed to try to get them to stop.

After a while I surprised myself by sitting down beside her and patting her back, something my mother used to do for me when I had an earache and was crying with pain. After a while Elspeth fell asleep.

After a while I did, too.

We were woken by the return of Spar Kellis. He came into the room carrying a covered tray that was tiny compared to him, enormous compared to us. I wondered if they had children in Dimension X and he had taken this tray from some poor kid's doll set.

"Time to eat!" he boomed cheerfully as he opened the door and thrust the tray into the cage.

I stared at it nervously. Given how weird this dimension was, the idea of eating was pretty scary.

Of course, not eating was even scarier.

Spar Kellis didn't wait to see if we enjoyed our meal. He turned away and disappeared through the left wall, leaving us on our own.

"What do you think?" asked Elspeth nervously. "Is it safe to eat?"

"Considering all the trouble they went through to get us here, I don't see why they'd bother to poison us," I replied. I didn't mention that I was ravenously hungry, which might have had some impact on my thinking.

Elspeth made a face. "I didn't *think* they were trying to poison us. But what if we just can't eat the food in this dimension? You know, like our bodies can't digest it, and it clogs up our intestines, and we get horribly bloated and explode or something? What if that happens?"

I remembered why I wasn't surprised that Aunt Grace and Uncle Roger had wanted to leave Elspeth with us for a while.

"What if we starve to death?" I replied.

"It wouldn't be as bad as exploding," said Elspeth, making a ghastly face.

I stared at the covered tray for a moment longer, then said, "Well, it can't hurt to look at it."

Now, if you've been on as many diets as I have, you know how this goes: You tell yourself you're just going to look at something, and next thing you know you're stuffing it in your face as fast as you can. I suspected that might happen this time. But I was too hungry to pay any attention to Elspeth's warnings—which were not totally stupid, even if they were unnecessarily grisly.

I tried to lift the lid from the tray. But though it was doll-size compared to Spar Kellis, it was still big enough to use for a Volkswagen hood in an emergency.

"Elspeth, give me a hand!"

"I don't think I should, Rod. If you eat that stuff and die and I ever get home alive, your mother would never forgive me."

"Elspeth," I snapped, "help me lift this thing or I can guarantee you'll never get home alive!"

I think I surprised myself as much as I did her. Cranky as Elspeth makes me, I had never actually yelled at her before. But then, I've hardly ever yelled at anyone. That's just not the way I am.

With an exaggerated sigh, she helped me lift the lid. Even though it looked like silver, it felt as if it was made of seaweed. "Yuck," said Elspeth, rubbing her hands against her jeans.

I didn't know if she was talking about the feel of the lid, or the look of the mess we found underneath.

CHAPTER
6

Dinner Conversation

I HAD TO ADMIT, IT WAS PRETTY REVOLTING—BASI-cally a pile of what looked like giant overcooked vegetables: soggy red spheres, leafy blue oblongs, and long snaky things that were probably roots of some sort. Or maybe they weren't. In this place, who could tell?

"I want a Twinkie," I said.

Elspeth was smirking. I think she had decided that she had won the point, and I wasn't going to eat anything after all. But hunger can lead you to do desperate things, and I realized it had been stupid to think that in Dimension X I was going to get something that looked like Mom's home cooking. So I picked up one of the red balls and took a bite.

"How is it?" asked Elspeth.

I am not proud of what I did then. Five weeks earlier, before I had learned to lie, I couldn't have done it even if I had wanted to. But after Elspeth's stomach-turning predictions about what might happen if we ate some of this stuff, I figured she had one coming. So instead of simply telling her that it was the worst thing I had ever tasted, something like a combination of chocolate and olives seasoned with mucus, I gave her a sickly grin and said, "Delicious!"

She looked at me suspiciously, but picked up one of the red spheres and sniffed at it.

Unfortunately for her, the smell gave no indication of how truly horrible this stuff was.

So she took a bite.

"Aaaaaagh!" she screamed, spitting it onto the floor of the cage. "That's disgusting, Rod!"

She began rubbing her mouth against her arm, trying to wipe out the taste.

I know, I know—it was a rotten thing for me to do. But I paid for it in the end. Since Elspeth refused to taste anything else on the tray, it was all up to me. As luck would have it, the horrible red spheres turned out to be the *best* tasting thing Spar Kellis had brought us. You can consider my refusing to describe what the rest of the meal tasted like as an act of mercy.

Well, at least I now knew one good thing about being stuck in Dimension X: It seemed likely that for the first time in my life I was going to be able to lose weight.

*   *   *

When Spar Kellis came to take our tray, he seemed annoyed that we had not done a better job on our meal.

"You two have to eat," he said, sounding a little nervous. "Smorkus Flinders has ordered me to keep you in good condition."

"I'd rather die than eat that stuff," said Elspeth.

Spar Kellis looked hurt. "I cooked it myself," he said, his voice quavering.

"It's just that it's not what we're used to," I said quickly.

Spar Kellis smiled. "Oh," he said. "Well, then it's just a matter of time. I'm sure you'll learn to love it."

Maybe he was right. Maybe if we had had a hundred years, we could have gotten used to that stuff. But I don't think so.

Fortunately, we didn't have to wait that long.

Things changed with the third meal that Spar Kellis brought us. As usual, we waited until he had left then lifted the lid and stared in despair at the meal. It looked pretty much like the last two messes he had brought us.

However, this time there was one major difference. While I was still trying to work up my courage to try a bit of something again, the meal started to move.

Jumping back, I watched in fascinated horror

as a snaky green tendril thrust out of the center of the pile and began shifting the other things around.

"Rod!" cried Elspeth, clutching my arm. "It's alive. *Our supper is alive!"*

"Alive and waiting for someone to lend a hand," burped a familiar voice.

"Phil!" I cried. "Phil, is that you?"

"Phil?" asked Elspeth, who was pressed against the bars on the far side of the cage again.

"Phillogenous esk Piemondum," I replied. "He's the Science Officer of the good ship *Ferkel!* At least, I think he's the Science Officer. Actually, I'm not sure exactly what he—"

"Are you going to help me out of this mess, or stand there and babble, young meat person?" interrupted Phil.

"Oh—sorry," I said. Stepping onto the tray, I shoved aside the vegetables and helped Phil to his roots.

"That's better," he said, using his tendrils to pluck bits and pieces of our dinner from his body. "Even though they were not sentient, I don't like being buried under things that in a better life might have been my cousins."

Unlike the first time I had met him, when he was only about two inches high, Phil was now full-size—which meant that he stood slightly higher than my waist. He had broad leaves and

more curling tendrils than I could count. His face (if he had a face) was hidden in the large yellow-orange blossom that grew at the top of his center stalk. Only one thing was different from the way I remembered him. . . .

"Your pot!" I cried. "Where's your pot?"

Phil usually traveled in a large pot that had rockets mounted on the bottom. Now I saw bare roots waving about at the base of his stalk. It made him look naked somehow.

"I had to remove myself from my pot in order to perform the deception that let me locate you."

I assumed that by "deception" he was referring to disguising himself as part of our dinner.

"Where are the others?" I asked.

"Coming soon, I hope," said Phil. "I am carrying a homing device which should allow them to locate us. With luck, they should arrive before much more time goes by." He paused, then asked, "Who is your companion?"

I wondered if he had seen her or only heard her. I really had no idea how Phil sensed things. His light sensors, if he had them, could have been located anywhere.

"This is my cousin, Elspeth."

"Greetings, Elspeth," said Phil.

"You're a plant!" said Elspeth.

This was none too intelligent, but no dumber than the things I had said when I first met Phil.

"And you're an animal," replied Phil. "Is this an issue for you?"

"But you're talking!"

"So are you."

"But you don't have a mouth!"

Curling a tendril, Phil drew aside a leaf to show one of the air pods that dangled from his inner stalk. "I use pod burps," he explained.

A blue face, small and furry, peered out from under another leaf and squeaked at us.

"You're infested!" gasped Elspeth.

"That's Plink," I said. "He's Phil's symbiote."

"His what?"

"They're a team. Plink runs and fetches for Phil. In return he gets to eat any branches, leaves, and nuts that Phil is done with."

Elspeth made a face. "That's sick!"

"Careful," I said in a whisper, "or he'll start telling you what parts of *human* biology are really disgusting."

"We have no time for a meaty discussion," said Phil. "We must prepare for the arrival of the *Ferkel*."

"How are we supposed to prepare?" I asked. "It's not like we have to pack or anything."

"Prepare *mentally*," burped Phil. "Be ready for rapid action."

Yeah, and stay calm, too, I thought.

And then there wasn't any more time to think, because the *Ferkel* came through the wall.

My joy at seeing the ship was cut short by the fact that the world suddenly went crazy. A burst of pink light filled the room. A high-pitched whine sliced through the air. The walls began to waver and change color.

And Elspeth grew tentacles.

CHAPTER
7

Reality Quake

ELSPETH BEGAN TO SHRIEK. FLASHES OF PINK LIGHT continued to erupt in the room. The whine got higher and shriller.

"What's going on?" I cried in horror, even as I backed away from Elspeth's writhing, lashing tentacles.

"Reality Quake," burped Phil.

I noticed that the *Ferkel* was tumbling end over end. It seemed to be going backward and forward at the same time, which didn't make any sense, but somehow didn't surprise me, given everything else that was happening.

"What's a Reality Quake?" shrieked Elspeth, who was about a foot taller than she had been a minute before. She was also turning green. I wondered what *I* looked like now, then decided that I didn't want to know.

Phil raised his blossom, and I saw behind his petals for the first time.

He had Elspeth's face!

"A Reality Quake is a Dimension X natural disaster," he said, shifting his feet—not his roots, his *feet!*—as the floor of our cage began to bubble. "It is like an earthquake on your world, except that what shifts is not the earth, but reality itself."

"How long does it last?" I cried. I was now half the size of Phil and Elspeth, but things were happening so fast I couldn't figure out if that was because they were growing or I was shrinking.

"No telling," said Phil. "Sometimes just a few minutes. Sometimes a few weeks."

Weeks? I thought in horror as I dwindled past Elspeth's knees.

Elspeth asked the more important question: "Is it permanent?" she screamed, waving her green tentacles in front of her face.

"Not usually," said Phil.

Then he split down the middle and began to melt.

Just as suddenly as it had begun, the Reality Quake was over. Phil snapped into his natural form. Elspeth's tentacles retracted into her body. I shot back up to my regular height.

"Ohmigod," gasped Elspeth. "That was the worst thing that's ever happened to me."

I didn't say anything. The Reality Quake had made me extremely queasy, and I was busy trying not to throw up.

Plink was shrieking and leaping from branch to branch of Phil's body. I couldn't blame the poor little guy.

Before I could begin to think of what to do next, the *Ferkel* landed on the table next to us. It was strange: The last time I had seen the *Ferkel* on a table, it had been my own table, and the *Ferkel* had been slightly larger than a football. Now it was full-size, but given the fact that the table it had landed on belonged to Smorkus Flinders, it appeared to be no bigger than it had when it first landed in my vat of papier-mâché that spring.

A ramp extended from the side of the ship.

Out stepped Grakker. Like Phil, he stood only slightly higher than my waist. Unlike Phil, he was a "meat person." He looked just as I remembered him: body like a bulked-up Greek statue, face like King Kong (if you don't count the green skin and nubby horns) and an expression that made you think he had just smelled something unpleasant and was trying to figure out who had done it.

"Deputy Allbright," he roared. "How in the name of the Seven Stars of Singala did you get yourself into this mess?"

While I didn't appreciate him yelling at me, I

did appreciate that he was simultaneously using his ray gun to melt the lock on our cage door. I wasn't sure if he was expecting me to answer or not.

Elspeth leaped in. "It wasn't our fault!" she shouted. "This monster just came out of nowhere and—"

"Silence!" bellowed Grakker. "Escape first, talk later."

This seemed sensible to me. As soon as Grakker finished melting the lock, he yanked open the cage door. Elspeth and I sprang for it. As I was passing through, Grakker fixed me with a furious glare. "Deputy Allbright, abandoning a comrade in the line of duty violates Galactic Patrol Guideline 1047.38.762. The penalties can be severe."

At first I didn't know what he was talking about. Then it hit me. Turning, I saw Phil struggling to follow us out of the cage. Since he didn't have his pot, he had to walk on his roots, which made his progress very slow indeed. I blushed with shame. "I didn't think—"

"You rarely do!" snapped Grakker.

Before he could say anything else, I darted back to help Phil. It wasn't easy, because I wasn't sure how to do it. If he had been a human being, I would have slipped an arm around his shoulder. But he didn't have a shoulder—just a stem, a blossom, and a lot of leaves. I might even have scooped him into my arms, since he was small enough for me to carry, but I wasn't sure how he felt about being touched.

"How . . . how can I help?" I stammered.

"Stand in front of me," burped Phil. "I will climb onto your back."

I did as he asked. It felt weird to have his tendrils grab my shoulders, and even weirder when he pulled himself up and wrapped his roots around my waist. But the reason Phil didn't have his pot to begin with was that he had abandoned it to rescue me, so it would have been really ungrateful to complain. (As my mother sometimes points out, I may be clumsy, but I'm polite.)

Once he was in place he burped softly, "Do not let Grakker's anger bother you. I am not offended by what you did. After all, you are not a trained member of the Galactic Patrol."

His words made me feel better and worse at the same time. While I was glad Phil was not offended, I didn't really want to be a young fool, either.

I didn't have time to worry about such things. Our main job at the moment was to escape. Moving slowly but steadily forward, I carried Phil through the cage door, past Grakker, to the ramp of the *Ferkel*. Elspeth had already gone into the ship. Grakker followed us.

Waiting inside was the rest of the crew: Madame Pong, the tall, elegant diplomatic officer; four-legged Tar Gibbons, the Master of the Martial Arts; and Flinge Iblik, sometimes known as Snout because of his long face, who was the Master of the Mental Arts. Though I was incredibly glad to see them, we had no time to greet each other. We had to get out of the home of Smorkus Flinders.

The moment the ramp had pulled in behind us and the door closed, Snout pushed a button that set the ship into motion.

Madame Pong and Tar Gibbons helped Phil down from my back and into his pot. Once his roots were safely tucked in place, he scooted over to join Snout at the control panel.

Madame Pong turned to me. Putting her yellow hands together, she made a little bow and murmured, "I welcome your return to the *Ferkel,* Rod Allbright."

I bowed back. Then, remembering that Madame Pong took great store in proper form, I said, "Allow me to present my cousin, Elspeth McMasters."

Elspeth looked at me in astonishment, as if she couldn't believe it was possible for me to do something polite. But she bowed to Madame Pong and said, "Very pleased to meet you."

Long neck stretching, Tar Gibbons scurried over to greet us. I was going to introduce it to Elspeth, but instead I fell over. This was not due to my old problem of basic clumsiness. I fell over because the ship had suddenly lurched wildly to the right.

"What was that?" roared Grakker.

"We're under attack," burped Phil.

The ship lurched again, this time to the left.

"What sort of attack?" asked Grakker.

"Fists," replied the plant. "It's Smorkus Flinders. He's hitting us!"

The ship lurched a third time, then shot forward.

"We've eluded him," reported Snout. "And we have escaped from Castle Chaos."

We all began to cheer.

Our joy was short-lived. The *Ferkel* began to slow down.

"We've sustained damage," reported Phil. "I can't get her to move."

"Where's the damage?" asked Grakker. "What will it take to repair it?"

"In the aft section," said Phil. Uncurling a green tendril, he pushed a button, lighting up a view screen.

"Uh-oh," he burped.

He didn't have to explain what the problem was. We could all see the screen.

Smorkus Flinders was coming after us, coming fast.

Grakker looked furious. But he didn't hesitate. "No time for repairs," he said. "We'll have to abandon ship."

CHAPTER
8

Ground Level

I COULDN'T BELIEVE GRAKKER WAS GOING TO ABANdon the *Ferkel*, but that may have been because I had watched too many episodes of "Star Trek."

Flinge Iblik, his long face trembling, handed me something that looked familiar. I examined it more closely and realized it was a flying belt, the same kind I had worn the last time I worked with the aliens.

"I trust you remember how to use this," he said, winking at me as I strapped it on.

I didn't know if it was *possible* for me to forget. Snout himself had taught me, using a mind-to-mind data transfer that nearly blew out his mental sockets when I unexpectedly broke the connection. I blushed at the memory of how I had come so close to permanently injuring him.

"No time now to train your cousin," said Phil. "She will have to ride with you."

Elspeth and I looked at each other uneasily. But just as there was no time to train her, there was no time for us to worry about little things.

"Climb on my back, as if we were playing piggyback," I said. "Get high enough so that you're above the belt."

She nodded, and did as I said. It would have been easier if I could have held her in my arms, but I needed my hands free to manipulate the controls.

Grakker had already opened the door of the ship. The others were lined up, ready to leave. He turned and saluted the empty cabin. "Farewell, my fine *Ferkel*," he said solemnly. "I swear I will return for you." Turning back to the crew, he snapped, "All right, everybody out! Try to stay close. Someone give Deputy Allbright a homing device. We'll gather on the ground as soon as we are able. Tar Gibbons, you first. Madame Pong, follow him."

As Grakker spoke the aliens began to leave the ship. After Madame Pong, Grakker called for me. With Elspeth on my back, I stepped up to the door. Looking down, I saw that we were about fifty feet above some of the macaroni-looking stuff Smorkus Flinders had waded through when he carried Elspeth and me to Castle Chaos.

I hesitated, then jumped.

I might have hesitated longer, but I spotted Smorkus Flinders racing toward us.

Elspeth and I plummeted downward, until I managed to adjust the belt's controls to handle both of us. The belt kicked in and stopped our fall just above the macaroni stuff. Though I didn't want to go into it, Tar Gibbons and Madame Pong had already disappeared beneath the surface. Phil shot past us, waving his leaves at me to follow.

Hoping we would be able to breathe in the stuff, I filled my lungs and plunged in.

It was utterly weird. The macaroni-like tubes slid and slithered around us almost as if they were alive.

"Rod," whispered Elspeth. "I hate this stuff."

"Me, too," I replied. Not that there was anything I could do about it.

At least the tubes were not closely packed. There was plenty of air surrounding them, and we could breathe comfortably. I wondered what held them up.

Down we went. It was hard to gauge how far we had to go. I assumed the stuff was piled about as high as Smorkus Flinders's waist (which is to say, about forty feet). But was there ground below it, or did the tubes simply became more and more densely packed, until they were solid enough to walk on?

A moment later I had my answer. We emerged from the macaroni stuff into a clear space about ten feet deep. At the bottom of the space was ground—or at least what passed for ground here in Dimension X. Tar Gibbons, Madame Pong, and Phil cheered when they saw us break through, and motioned for us to join them. As we touched down, I looked up. The macaroni stuff, as close as a ceiling, stretched on as far as I could see in every direction. I wondered if it always stayed at the same level, or if sometimes it got lower, even settled to the ground like some weird fog bank. I shivered at the thought of having to walk through it.

As Elspeth was climbing down from my shoulders, Flinge Iblik landed beside us, followed closely by Grakker.

"All together at last," said Madame Pong happily.

Grakker snorted. "All together only because we have been forced to come here to rescue Deputy Allbright. By allowing himself to be captured by Smorkus Flinders, he has endangered our entire crew."

I started to protest, but Snout beat me to it. "Ah, my mighty captain, had you not offended Smorkus Flinders so badly that he was thirsting for revenge, perhaps the problem would never have occurred in the first place."

Grakker wrinkled his face, but said nothing. I had noticed that he would take criticism from Snout that he would accept from no one else. I also wondered just how he had "offended" Smorkus Flinders.

This didn't seem like the time to ask.

"Blame is not important," said Madame Pong. "The important thing is to decide what to do next."

"What we must do next is finish escaping," said Tar Gibbons.

Indeed, somewhere above us we could hear Smorkus Flinders bellowing in rage at losing sight of us. Before any of us could suggest what to do about completing our escape, the ground shook as if with a minor earthquake. I was looking past Madame Pong, and I cried out in horror when I saw the cause. Smorkus Flinders had thrown himself to his stomach and was lying with his head pressed to the ground, staring straight at us. With a cry of satisfaction he thrust his arm in our direction. His fingers came within inches of me.

"Fly!" shouted Madame Pong.

I needed no urging. The instincts Snout had installed in my brain, the automatic instructions for manipulating the flying belt, took over and I launched myself away from those groping orange fingers. Grakker himself snatched up Elspeth. "Follow me!" he shouted.

Traveling about five feet above the ground, halfway to the macaroni stuff, we flew away.

Smorkus Flinders roared in frustration. His size worked against him now, because the only way he could keep us in sight was by slithering along on his belly with his head pressed to the ground. If he rose even to his knees to pursue us, he would be blinded by the strange atmosphere.

With Grakker in the lead, we made a quarter circle around our enemy, then flew straight away from him. After a time his cries of anger grew faint behind us. Grakker kept flying for another half hour or so, then motioned for us to land.

We gathered in a knot on the ground. It was spongy feeling, as if we were standing on a giant mushroom. Our joy at escaping from Smorkus Flinders was tempered by the fact that we were lost in one of the five strangest dimensions in the Pandimensionality.

For a moment no one spoke. Elspeth came to stand beside me. Her eyes wide, she was staring at the aliens.

Finally Grakker turned to Madame Pong. "Do we have any allies in this place?" he asked.

Madame Pong pulled a wire from the silvery band that circled her wrist. With one end of the wire still connected to her wrist, she inserted the other end into her ear and closed her eyes. After a moment she shook her head and said, "We have no formal alliances here."

Grakker snorted, as if dismissing all diplomats

for this failure. Turning to Snout, he said, "See if you can locate a friendly presence."

"With pleasure, my captain," said Snout. Wrapping his long blue cape around him, the lizard-faced alien settled to a cross-legged position and closed his eyes. I started to ask what he was doing, but a look from Madame Pong cautioned me to silence.

Suddenly Snout's eyes flew open. Leaping to his feet, he cried out in terror. Then his eyes rolled back in his head, his body grew stiff, and he fell to the ground, where he lay as if dead.

CHAPTER
9

Wherefore Art Thou, Snout?

FASTER THAN I COULD BLINK MY EYES, GRAKKER WAS kneeling at Snout's side. Tenderly he lifted one of his friend's eyelids and stared into the motionless eye. Then he held a hand in front of Snout's tapered purple-brown face. After a moment he turned to the rest of us and grunted, "He's alive."

"What happened to him?" asked Elspeth nervously.

Grakker wrinkled his nose. "I do not know. In his search for friends, he must have encountered some great evil instead."

"Or simply some great power," murmured Madame Pong.

"Possible," said Grakker grudgingly.

Elspeth looked puzzled. "What do you mean, 'his search for friends'?"

65

"Snout is the Master of the Mental Arts," I answered excitedly. "He can do things with his brain that you can hardly imagine. Once I actually felt him slow down time!"

Elspeth looked at me as if she thought something had gone seriously wrong with my own brain. Maybe she was right. If my brain was working properly, I would have read more of that book Snout had given me when I had the chance. Why hadn't I done that? At first I had been eager to read it, but for a while I was so wound up from our adventure that I hadn't been able to concentrate. Then I had just let it slide, figuring I could do it later. Now I couldn't believe how many nights I had wasted watching TV instead of reading that book. Dumb. Dumb, dumb, dumb.

"Look!" said Madame Pong. "He's moving!"

Twitching would have been a more precise word. As we all turned back to Snout, his body began to vibrate like a plucked rubber band. Suddenly he turned clear, then began to fade. Soon he was little more than a ghostly image of himself.

"No!" cried Grakker, throwing himself across Snout's chest.

Alas, the captain's great strength was no match for whatever was happening. A moment later Snout had vanished completely.

Pushing himself to his knees, Grakker raised his head to the boiled macaroni sky and howled in rage and sorrow. Suddenly he turned toward me and roared, "Deputy Allbright, this is entirely your fault!"

I was long used to Grakker shouting at me. But when he actually took a step toward me as if he were about to throttle me, I got nervous. Fortunately, Madame Pong stepped in. Slipping up behind him, she pulled something about the size of a half-used pencil from the back of his head. Moving quickly, she inserted another in its place.

Glancing around Grakker's massive shoulder, she said apologetically, "I hadn't had a chance to change modules yet. He was still in full battle mode."

"You know, of course, that I believe that battle module to be badly programmed," said Tar Gibbons, blinking its huge eyes in disapproval. "Warrior Science demands self control, not mindless rage."

Stepping around Grakker, Madame Pong said, "I have noted your complaints and forwarded them to the appropriate authorities many times, Tar Gibbons."

"Where's Snout?" asked Elspeth, asking the only question that mattered at this point. "What happened to Snout?"

"He has been stolen from us," said Grakker. His voice was fierce but controlled, and I wondered what module Madame Pong had inserted in his head. "How this was managed, I do not know. But I swear by Zarkov's Ray Gun that we will do all in our power to get him back." He turned to Madame Pong. "Are you aware of anyone—any power, any technology—that could have done this?"

"Let me check the data banks," she said, pulling the silvery wire from her wrist band once again.

Grakker turned his attention to Phil and Tar Gibbons. "I ask you the same question: Who or what could have taken our shipmate?"

The Tar blinked its big eyes. "I know of no one who has such a power. But let us consider an alternative possibility. Could this disappearance be something the Mental Masters do automatically under certain circumstances—for example, if Snout's vital symptoms dropped to a certain level, is it not possible he might have preset his body to do what it just did?"

"Possible, but unlikely," said Madame Pong, withdrawing the wire from her ear. "Not that he couldn't have done such a thing. But if that were the case, he would have prepared us to expect such a disappearance. No, this is clearly some outside force. The question is, is it the work of an enemy or simply some factor of life in Dimension X that we are not aware of? Whatever did it," she added, turning to Grakker, "it is not something that appears in the data banks."

"Perhaps it was one of the higher secrets of the Mental Masters," burped Phil. "One that Snout could not speak of, even to us."

"Which leaves us right back where we started," said Tar Gibbons.

"A place in which we cannot remain," said Grakker resolutely. "We must find food, shelter, and assistance."

I looked at him in surprise. I had half expected him to insist that we would stay where we were until we located Snout. But since Snout could have been anywhere in Dimension X—or out of it, for that matter—I realized that that wouldn't make sense.

Unfortunately nothing else seemed to make any sense, either. We had nothing to indicate one direction would be any better than another, not a single clue to guide us. I don't think it is possible to be more lost than we were at the time.

"I could try putting down roots," said Phil.

Grakker frowned. "I do not want to risk another crew member."

"Warrior Science says when there is no other choice, make the choice that is possible," said Tar Gibbons.

Grakker paused, then nodded. "All right," he said to Phil. "Try."

Phil climbed out of his pot. I moved closer to Madame Pong. Leaning down, I whispered into her large, pointed ear, "What's he doing?"

"He is going to try to penetrate the soil with his roots. By doing so, he may be able to gather information from other plants."

"What are the odds that there will be intelligent plants here?" I asked. Even though Phil acted offended whenever someone was surprised by meeting an intelligent plant, the fact that he was the only one on the crew seemed to indicate that his type of being was not all that common.

Tar Gibbons had overheard me. "Something does not have to be intelligent in order to offer information," it said, stretching its long neck in order to speak directly into my ear. "If Phil can tap into the plant web, he may be able to sense things that can lead us to centers of population; even tell us which ones, if any, are good places for us to go."

"What kind of things?" asked Elspeth.

The Tar blinked its baseball-sized eyes. "Chemical traces of life activity. Signs of the interaction between being and environment. For example, soil enriched by respect or depleted by carelessness. Phil can read these things, even at a distance."

I thought I understood, and turned to watch Phil. He had spread his roots around him in an even pattern. They were arched and stiff, almost as if he was flexing them, so that they held his main stem a few inches above the ground. The tips of the roots were tapping, tapping, tapping at the soil. The rest of his body was perfectly still, and I could tell he was focusing all his attention, all his energy, on the roots.

He tapped harder and harder.

His leaves began to quiver.

I was wondering if this was a sign of frustration when a voice behind me said, in very cranky tones, "Just *what* do you think you're doing?"

CHAPTER
10

Out of Shape

I SPUN AROUND TO SEE WHO WAS SPEAKING, THEN stumbled backward in astonishment.

The ground was looking at me. Well, actually it was probably looking at Phil. In either case, the effect was pretty startling.

When I say it was looking at us, I mean exactly that. The soil, or whatever, had *opened an eye* about two feet from where I had been standing. I glanced around nervously, wondering if I would see eyes opening all over the place. To my relief, this was the only one.

"What do you think you're doing?" repeated the voice.

Grakker started to say something, but Madame Pong held up a long-fingered hand to silence him. "We humbly beg your pardon," she said, making a little bow in the direction of the eye. "We were seeking assistance."

72

"Why?"

"We are fleeing from someone who wishes to harm us."

The eye blinked. "Who?" asked the voice.

"That is classified information," said Grakker gruffly. "Do not answer, Madame."

"Objection overruled," said Madame Pong.

A dangerous rumble started low in Grakker's throat.

"We are not on the ship now, Captain," said Madame Pong smoothly. "This is a diplomatic matter, and I have jurisdiction." Turning back to the eyeball, she said, "We are being sought by a creature named Smorkus Flinders."

I wondered if she was making a big mistake. What if the eyeball was working for Smorkus Flinders? Maybe it could contact him instantly and tell him where we were. But Madame Pong's diplomatic instincts must have been right on target, because the eyeball blinked and said, "Ah, that changes things. I do not like Smorkus Flinders. I would be glad to help you, except for the fact that you are standing on me, and your friend has been trying to drill a hole through my flesh."

Feeling guilty, I glanced down at my feet. I would have moved, but I didn't know where to go so that I *wouldn't* be standing on the guy. For all I knew, we were talking to the whole planet— assuming they actually had planets in Dimension X.

73

Madame Pong asked the question for me. "Where would you like us to move?"

"If you would all take about ten paces backward, I would appreciate it," replied the voice.

I glanced over my shoulder, then backed away. Muttering to himself, waving his tendrils, Phil climbed into his pot and floated over to join the rest of us.

"Thank you," said the voice, which seemed to come from underneath us, though not from any specific spot.

As we watched, the ground suddenly began to ripple and flow, rising up and moving toward the eyeball like some speeded up educational film showing how mountains are formed. In a matter of seconds we saw the outline of a body. In less than a minute the eyeball—now encased in a complete body, including another eyeball—stood up. The body was stocky and slightly taller than Grakker and the crew, though still shorter than Elspeth or me. Its skin was the same color as the ground. At least, it started out that color. However, a few seconds after it had assumed its new shape it also changed color, becoming a deep maroon, almost purple.

It had no clothing, which I suppose made sense for something that could change shape that way; I mean, how could you expect the clothes to change with you? For a minute I wondered if I

should cover Elspeth's eyes, or tell her to look away. But since I couldn't tell whether the newcomer was a man or a woman myself (and from previous conversations with the aliens I knew that it was entirely possible that it was neither) I decided it did not make that much difference.

"Greetings," it said, touching a pudgy maroon hand to its forehead. "Galuspa Nosto Fingel Fingel Istenkeppel at your service. You may call me Galuspa."

"Greetings, Galuspa," replied Madame Pong, repeating the gesture. "Our apologies for having stood upon you."

"Quite all right," said the creature. "After all, if you had known *not* to stand on me, it would have meant that my disguise was not working very well, don't you think?"

"Definitely," said Madame Pong.

The creature smiled. "It's effective, wouldn't you say? The disguise, I mean."

"Very," said Madame Pong. "Is it unique, or do others of your kind do the same thing?"

"Oh, we all take different shapes. But I like being the ground best. It does mean you get walked on occasionally. But you pretty much get ignored, too, which is the point of the whole thing, of course."

"Of course," said Madame Pong. "And I am sorry that we disturbed you. However, now that we have, perhaps you can indeed help us. Is there anywhere nearby that we can rest in safety, get some food, maybe even some assistance?"

Food. What a good idea. I was *starving!* Thirsty, too.

Our formerly flat friend looked at us carefully. "Exactly why is Smorkus Flinders after you?"

I wondered how Madame Pong would answer. Clearly this guy (I'm going to call him a guy for the sake of convenience) didn't like Smorkus Flinders. On the other hand, if he thought helping us might put him and his people in danger, maybe he would decide against it.

Madame Pong pointed to Elspeth and me. "Smorkus Flinders stole these children from their home in Dimension Q in order to lure us here."

(This was the first I knew that we lived in Dimension Q!)

"Why did he want to lure you here?" asked Galuspa.

Madame Pong was smooth. Nothing she did or said gave me a clue that she was holding back part of the story when she replied, "He is seeking vengeance because we tracked down and arrested a friend of his." It was the little growl in Grakker's throat and the way I could feel him tensing up beside me that reminded me of Snout's unfinished comment about the captain antagonizing Smorkus Flinders. I wondered what that was all about. I wondered if I would ever find out.

77

Galuspa made a gesture that I understood to mean that Madame Pong's answer made sense to him. "I can take you to a place where you will be safer than you are now," he said. "How safe, I cannot guarantee. As long as Smorkus Flinders rules this place, no one can be sure of anything."

"I wanna go home!" said Elspeth. "This minute!"

"We gratefully accept your assistance," murmured Madame Pong as I tried to glare my cousin into silence.

Galuspa looked at Elspeth and turned his whole body into a giant head with a big frown. I couldn't tell if he was being sympathetic, or making fun of her.

"Stop it!" snapped Elspeth, stamping her foot. A weird look crossed her face and she glanced at the ground nervously, suddenly afraid she had whalloped one of Galuspa's relatives.

"Has she been eating well?' asked the shapeshifter, snapping back into his regular form. "She sounds as if she's constipated."

Before Elspeth could come up with a reply to this—and I could tell she was working on one—Madame Pong laid a warning hand on her shoulder. Though her touch appeared to be gentle, Elspeth got the message, since she managed to keep her mouth shut. Which was just as well, since I had the impression that Galuspa's question was sincere and not a wisecrack.

"None of us are doing well at the moment," said Madame Pong softly.

Galuspa nodded. "Follow me. I will do what I can."

When he turned and began to walk away I noticed that his shape changed slightly with each step that he took—bulging out here or there, then snapping back into place, as if his edges were not that firm.

We hesitated, and I knew we were all thinking the same thing: Maybe we should not leave this place without Snout. But after a moment Grakker grunted and began to walk. The rest of us followed him.

Though the land had appeared flat at first, I began to realize that it curved gently up and down. The ground remained soft and spongy— usually just soft enough to be easy on the feet, but sometimes so soft that it was actually hard to walk. It was multicolored, the colors in the form of large, irregular patches that were quite distinct from each other, so that we might walk for ten or fifteen feet over a patch of orange ground and then come to a patch of lime green. It was odd, but sort of pretty. I kept wondering if the patches were Galuspa's relatives.

Two things made the landscape even stranger. First, there did not seem to be any plants; the ground was bare and smooth in all directions.

Second, the boiled macaroni "sky" curved to match the ground, so that whether we were going uphill or down, it was always the same distance above us.

As we walked, Galuspa told us about his people: how they preferred hiding to fighting, but could be very fierce when provoked; how much they hated Smorkus Flinders; and how they used ladders to pull the macaroni stuff (which they called *kispa-dinka*) out of the sky so that they could eat it.

I wondered if the macaroni stuff was actually some sort of plant life. I was walking along, staring up at it and trying to figure this out, when I fell into a hole.

I'm used to stumbling like that; they don't call me Rod the Clod for nothing.

What I'm not used to is once I've fallen down having some furry thing leap onto my back and then wrap itself around my head.

CHAPTER
11

The Chibling

PANIC SWEPT THROUGH MY BODY. "GET IT OFF!" I cried. *"Whatever it is, get it off me!"*

"Eeep!" shrieked the thing on top of me. "Eeep! Eeep!"

I reached up and tried to grab it, then pulled my hands back. So far the thing was only holding on to my head. What if when I tried to pull it off it decided to bite me? I had a sudden fear of catching the Dimension X version of rabies or something.

Because this was so sudden, because I had no idea what had grabbed me, I think I was even more frightened than when Smorkus Flinders had picked me up. At least I had been able to *see* him.

Galuspa came to my rescue. "Uh-oh," he said, sounding amused. "Looks like you've found a chibling."

"I didn't find anything!" I yelled. "It found me. Get it off!"

"Certainly," said Galuspa.

Muttering quietly, as if to reassure the thing, he pried it away from my head.

For a moment I lay with my face against the ground. I patted the back of my head, trying to discover if any of my skull had been removed, or melted, or anything like that. When I decided that it felt normal I rolled over. Galuspa stood there smiling at me. Nestled in his arms was a ball of purple fur the size of a watermelon. I was a little annoyed to realize that I had been terrified by something that looked like a carnival prize.

"Here," said Galuspa, holding the creature out to me. "Your chibling."

"It's not mine," I replied. I decided against standing up until we had this worked out.

"It is now," replied the shapeshifter firmly.

A little alarm bell went off in my head. "What do you mean by that?"

"It's bonded to you," said Galuspa. "Emotionally attached. Doesn't take them long to do that, for some reason. If you leave it behind now, it will mourn helplessly for weeks. It won't eat or sleep. Eventually it will die."

Great. One more thing to feel guilty about.

A large eyeball appeared in the mass of purple fur, then another. "Eeep!" said the chibling, struggling to get out of Galuspa's arms. "Eeep! Eeep! Eeep!"

"Is there any way to get it to bond with something else?" I asked as it broke free and came hurtling toward me.

"It's possible, but not easy," said Galuspa.

The chibling wrapped itself around my leg and began to make a high-pitched humming noise. Though the noise itself was pretty, I had been around enough dogs to get nervous when an animal attaches itself to my leg that way. "What's it doing?" I cried in alarm.

"What do you mean?" asked Galuspa.

"That sound. What is it?"

"It probably just means that it's happy," said Elspeth. "Like it's purring or something."

"I do not know what purring means," said Galuspa, "but the sound is indeed one of happiness. It means that it is glad to have found you. Once chiblings reach second stage, they must find a sentient creature to bond with. It is their first life task."

"I want one," said Elspeth.

"You can have this one," I said, giving my leg a shake.

The chibling shrieked and tightened its grip.

"Or maybe not," I said with a sigh.

"I want one!" repeated Elspeth.

"Actually, that would be a bad idea," said Galuspa.

"Why?" asked Elspeth.

"The more you have, the dumber they get, at least while in second stage."

"What does *that* mean?" I asked.

"You three can discuss the psychological development of chiblings later," interrupted Grakker, who had been watching this scene with growing impatience. "Right now I would rather continue our trip. I wish to have the crew in a place of safety so that we can begin considering our next moves. Can you walk with that thing attached to your leg, Deputy Allbright?"

I stood up and took a few steps. "I think so."

"It won't be necessary for long," said Galuspa. "Once the chibling realizes you're not trying to get rid of it, it will let go and run along beside you."

"How will it know I'm not trying to get rid of it?"

"It will know."

"Do you mean it will read my mind?" I asked in alarm.

Galuspa paused, as if he was trying to figure out how to answer this. "It will read your *intentions*," he said at last. "It's not as if it can understand your every thought. But it will have a sense of what you intend to do in regard to itself. As soon as you stop thinking about getting rid of it, it will let go by itself and be content to walk beside you."

This was like telling you that a toothache would go away if you would just stop thinking about it. The more you *try* to stop, the more your mind dwells on it.

"Let's go," I sighed.

Grakker grunted with satisfaction. We began to move again, me walking with my legs spread awkwardly apart to make room for the chibling.

"I want one," said Elspeth again.

"You do not!" I snapped.

"Yes, I do," she said. "Because I wouldn't be thinking about trying to get rid of it, so it wouldn't hold on to me so tightly."

"Well, I'd give you this one if I could!" I said angrily, holding up my foot. Naturally, the chibling tightened its grip on my leg and began to whimper.

Elspeth made a pouty face. "You get everything," she said. Then she went to walk beside Madame Pong.

I wish Snout was still here, I thought as I thumped along, swinging my right leg in a half circle in order not to knock the chibling against my left leg. *He could probably teach me a way to stop thinking about this thing so that it would let go of me.*

Of course, thinking about Snout made me sad and worried, because I wondered what had happened to him. It also got me thinking about the book he had given me that I had not read, except for that first page that said, "Stay calm."

I started repeating that to myself as I walked along. "Stay calm, Rod. Stay calm, Rod," I muttered over and over again.

I don't know how long I had been doing that before I realized that the chibling had gotten off my leg, and was moving along beside me. It traveled with an odd kind of flowing motion. Its fur brushed against the ground, and I could not tell how many legs it had. Both its eyes were visible now—they were about the size of Ping-Pong balls and bulged out from the front of its head.

The first thought that came to mind was that if I ran fast enough, maybe I could ditch the thing. I tried to push the thought out of my head, fearing that if the chibling picked it up, it would immediately wrap itself around my leg again.

I stopped.

The chibling stopped.

I got down on my knees.

The chibling stood up, making us nearly face-to-face. Except for the fact that it was about a foot and a half tall, it looked a little like a caterpillar does when it raises its front end. I could see several pairs of little black legs sticking out from under the purple fur.

I felt an urge to pet it, but was frightened of what might happen if I tried. Would it bite me?

Wrap itself around my arm? Inject me with some weird Dimension X venom?

I decided to keep my hands to myself.

"Eeep?" it asked pleadingly.

"Oh . . . eeep!" I replied at last. "Look, buddy, I hate to tell you this, but the truth is, I'm not planning on staying in Dimension X, and I don't think you'd be happy where I come from. So you might want to attach yourself to someone else when you get the chance."

"*Eeeeeeeeeep!*" it cried in dismay.

I wondered if it had really understood me or simply picked up on the general idea that I was suggesting it find someone else. Whatever the reason, it began to tremble as if it had caught a terrible chill.

"Rod!" said Elspeth. "You stop being mean to that poor thing or I'll tell your mother on you!"

"My mother's not here!" I snapped.

I regretted my outburst immediately—not only because of the look that passed over Elspeth's face, but because it made me realize that my words to the chibling about leaving it behind when I went home were only so much talk. At the moment the odds of getting home looked pretty slim.

Moreover, those words brought to mind my other major worry, namely how my mother was dealing with our disappearance. If only there was some way I could get a message to her!

"Keep moving!" shouted Grakker, from ahead of us.

Galuspa turned himself into a wheel and came rolling back. His face was located in the center, sort of like a hubcap. "We're almost there," he said. "Best not to delay at this point."

"All right, all right," I said. "I'm coming as fast as I can!"

"Eeeep!" said the chibling.

"We're coming," I corrected.

"Good," said Galuspa. Then he rolled off to the front of the group.

The low-hanging macaroni sky was moaning and whining above us. It was starting to get dark, which was the first time that I realized that I had no idea where the light was coming from to begin with.

We crested a small hill and found a dozen or so of Galuspa's people on the other side.

Thank goodness, I thought. *At least we'll be safe for the time being.*

That thought vanished when they all pulled out ray guns and pointed them at us. Galuspa, who was now in his regular shape, said, "Please do not resist. I do not want to have to harm any of you."

CHAPTER
12

The Valley of the Shapeshifters

"TREACHERY!" GROWLED GRAKKER. HE WAS TALKING to Galuspa, but from the look he shot Madame Pong, I could tell he was thinking that as Diplomatic Officer she should have seen this coming and kept us out of it.

"Not actually," said Galuspa. "Think of it as a safety measure. Those of us working for the overthrow of Smorkus Flinders cannot be too careful. Treachery does indeed lurk all around us. If we are to take you into our sanctuary, we must be sure that you really are fugitives and not part of that treachery."

"We came upon you while fleeing Smorkus Flinders," said Madame Pong. "What better sign of good faith can we offer?"

"That is not up to me to say," replied Galuspa.

"You will have to discuss the matter with the Ting Wongovia."

"What's a Ting Wongovia?" whispered Elspeth while the newcomers took Grakker's ray gun and checked the rest of us for weapons.

"I don't have the slightest idea," I whispered back.

I felt a weight on my foot and realized that the chibling had wrapped itself around me again. "Coward," I muttered, shaking my leg. The chibling only *eeeped* and clung tighter than ever.

We started out again, surrounded by the shapeshifters. I kept expecting Grakker to lead a break for freedom by using his flying belt to soar into the macaroni sky. When he didn't, I tried to figure out why not, and came up with three possibilities: (a) the shapeshifters were all carrying ray guns and could probably zap us instantly; (b) we still had no idea where we were, and at least our captors were taking us *someplace;* or (c) he actually believed that we (or, more likely, Madame Pong) could convince these people that we were on their side against Smorkus Flinders.

The fourth possibility was that he just didn't have time to make a break for it. We had only climbed two more small hills before we came to one of those floating ovals Smorkus Flinders had kept stepping through when he took Elspeth and

me to his home. This one was much smaller—
no more than seven feet high. Someone as tall
as Smorkus Flinders wouldn't even have seen it
hidden beneath the macaroni sky.

"We have to go through here," said Galuspa,
waving his ray gun toward the oval. "Three of
my people will go first. Then we'll alternate—
one of you, one of us—until we're all on the
other side."

Three of the shapeshifters immediately jumped
through the oval and disappeared. Galuspa
pointed his ray gun at Grakker and said, "Now
you."

Grakker snarled, but jumped through the oval.

He was followed immediately by one of the
shapeshifters.

"Next you," said Galuspa, pointing to Phil.

Phil guided his pot to the oval. With a sudden
burst of energy from the rockets at the pot's base,
he shot up and disappeared over the edge. Since
the bottom of the oval came to about her knees,
Madame Pong used her flying belt to get through.
Tar Gibbons, however, simply jumped.

A shapeshifter followed each of them.

When they had all gone through, Galuspa
pointed his ray gun at me and nodded.

"See you on the other side," I said to Elspeth.
Swallowing nervously, I approached the oval.
Stepping over an edge that was knee height to

Madame Pong was easy for me, of course. Even so, I hesitated. While I had been through several of these things already, I still didn't like the idea. What if it malfunctioned, and I ended up nowhere at all? What if it brought me out in midair, and I ended up plunging to my doom?

Reminding myself that I had a flying belt, I stepped through . . . and began to smile. After the strange desolation through which we had been traveling, the place to which Galuspa had brought us was almost unbearably beautiful. Weird, of course; we *were* still in Dimension X, after all. But beautiful nonetheless.

No longer did the boiled macaroni sky hang oppressively over our heads. Now the sky was clear and distant, as it should be. True, it was streaked with purple and green, and filled with large red balls traveling in slow circles. But at least I didn't feel like it was about to crush me.

Nor was the ground empty and bare. Things were growing here. What kind of things I couldn't say, other than that they were large and mushroomlike. But it was a relief to see some plant life again.

When I say large, by the way, I mean tree-size. The average "trunk" had a diameter about the same as my waist; the biggest ones were as big around as the Things' blow-up wading pool. Their spreading caps, which grew as much as a hundred feet above us, were easily large enough to make a roof for a good-size house—and indeed, when we traveled a little farther, it turned out that the people here used them for exactly that purpose. They came in a variety of colors, including three or four that I had never seen before. When I asked Phil how that was possible, he told me that light behaved differently in Dimension X than in our own world.

Things that looked like snakes with wings flitted among the tree.

The oval had deposited us on a broad hillside. Ahead of us a path wound gently down among the mushroom trees. Not far from where we stood the path crossed a little stream by means of a bridge. The bridge was yellow, but I could not tell what materials it was made from.

The stream reminded me of how thirsty I was.

I was still trying to take all this in when I was knocked over by the shapeshifter who came through the oval after me. I felt really stupid; I should have realized I would have to get out of his way. Elspeth arrived soon after, followed by the rest of the shapeshifters. Galuspa came through last.

"Home at last," he said. "Welcome to Laronda, the Valley of the Shapeshifters."

His voice was not simply cheerful. I would have to say it was *joyful*. Moving to the head of the group, he began to lead the way down the path.

"I'm thirsty," said Elspeth when we got to the bridge.

"You may drink," said Galuspa, gesturing toward the stream.

I was thirsty, too, but when I started to think about drinking that water, I realized that I was even more concerned about what it might do to us than Elspeth had been about eating the food earlier.

"Is it safe?" I asked Phil. (I asked Phil because he was the ship's Science Officer.)

Rather than answering me he turned to Galuspa and said, "May I sample the water?"

"If you must."

Phil guided his pot down to the stream, extended one of his roots, and dipped it into the water. After a moment he retracted the root. Gliding back up to the bridge, he said, "The chemical composition is exactly the same as water in our dimension. Taking into account several factors, I estimate that the chance of dangerous microorganisms is approximately two percent."

"Not high, but not as safe as I would like," said Grakker.

"Maybe we shouldn't drink it after all," I said nervously.

"Perhaps not," replied Phil. "However, the chances of death from dehydration should you have nothing to drink are, in the long run, one

hundred percent. As it seems unlikely that we will be able to return to the ship any time soon, it might be wise to drink now."

"Would it be possible to get sterile water where you are taking us?" Madame Pong said to Galuspa.

"This is what we drink," he said. "Besides, it is growing dark, and soon we must rest for the night. We are still another day's travel from our village."

Which pretty much decided the matter. One by one, under the watchful eye of the shapeshifters, we went to the stream and drank. The water was cool, clear, and delicious. Even so, I worried that I was going to catch some terrible Dimension X disease and die. (Several of the shapeshifters took the opportunity to drink, too, but I figured they would be used to whatever germs might live in the water, so that didn't make me feel any safer.)

We continued our journey, traveling up and down several hills. Though the path itself was bare, the forest floor on either side of it was covered with strange plants, including some red ones that made a constant humming noise.

"Hey," said Elspeth. "The hills really are alive with the sound of music!"

Finally Galuspa called a halt for the night. The shapeshifters prepared a meal, which turned out to be *kispa-dinka*, fried and mixed with something that looked like flower petals. Remembering the food we had been given in Castle Chaos, I stared at the meal for a long time before I finally got up the courage to taste it.

To my astonishment (and relief!) it was pretty good—sweet and slightly spicy. I ate three helpings of it.

When it was time to sleep the shapeshifters linked themselves together to form a fence around us. While I was trying to settle down Madame Pong came and sat next to me.

"Rod," she said softly. "I need to speak to you for a moment."

"About what?" I asked warily.

"I have done something that you need to be aware of."

"What do you mean?"

She looked directly into my eyes. "When we discovered that you had been taken to Dimension X, I took the liberty of sending your mother a letter."

"You did what?"

She put one of her long fingered hands on my arm, a request for me to stay calm.

"You must understand that we had no way of knowing how long it would take us to find you and return you to your home. Rather than have your mother wracked with worry about what might have happened to you, I gave her a reason for your absence."

I snorted. "You think telling my mother that I was kidnapped by a giant monster from Dimension X is going to make her stop worrying?"

Madame Pong smiled gently. "I didn't say I told her the truth, only that I gave her a reason for your absence."

I frowned, trying to imagine what reason Madame Pong could have invented for my absence that would have kept my mother from going berserk with worry. It was ridiculous; there was no such excuse.

Or so I thought.

"All right," I said. "What did you tell her?"

"I said that your father had taken you away for a visit, and that he would bring you back as soon as he was able."

I felt as if I had been punched in the stomach. I hadn't seen my father in nearly three years. Madame Pong's excuse was my secret daydream.

Taking a deep breath, I said, "I don't think that's going to make her much happier."

"Would you prefer that she be left with no hope, living in terror of what has happened to you?"

Since that was exactly what I had been worried about, I had to admit that Madame Pong's solution was at least a step in the right direction.

"I wrote the letter as from an anonymous friend of the family, assuring her that you would be well cared for, and that you would return before the end of the summer." She paused, then said softly, "I hope that we will be able to turn that much of the letter into the truth."

"It was kind of you," I said. "I appreciate it."

She shook her head. "It is not enough, but it was the best I could do on such short notice. We do have some ways to make it more believable. There will be some other clues and messages, things to help set your mother's mind at ease. In fact, later this week she will received a phone call from you."

"I can call home?" I cried, feeling a little like E.T.

Madame Pong looked distressed. "No, of course not."

But you said . . ."

"I'm sorry, Rod. I didn't mean to mislead you. What I meant was that recordings we have of your voice from the last time you were on the *Ferkel* will be used to synthesize a brief message to her, assuring her that you are well."

"Awesome!"

"Additionally, it is my hope that once things are in motion our agents will realize that Elspeth is with you, and weave her into the story they are creating to cover for your absence. Your mother won't be happy, but I think we can keep her from total panic.''

"Thank you," I said. "Thank you so much."

That night I slept soundly for the first time since I had been brought to Dimension X.

The next morning, after a breakfast of *kispa-dinka*, we set out again. When we had been walking for about an hour Tar Gibbons made a point of positioning itself beside me. At first this pleased me, because I admired the Tar, and wanted it to like me as well. But after a while I got the weird feeling that it was examining me—studying me for some reason.

At last we crested a steep hill and found ourselves looking down on Galuspa's village. I didn't realize it was a village at first because all the houses had roofs made from the tops of the mushroom trees, so it just looked like another forest until I realized that the "treetops" were much too close to the ground. Then I noticed the winding streets, and the people walking along them.

"Home at last," said Galuspa happily.

In the village we passed a group of children playing a game that seemed to consist of seeing who could twist their body into the weirdest shape. Just watching them made my bones ache, though I also found myself wishing that I could do the same thing. Turning myself into a chair would be a great way to hide from Thing One and Thing Two whenever I didn't want to play with them.

Thinking of the Things only made me realize how far I was from home, which only made me feel sorry for myself again.

The chibling seemed to sense my feelings, because it made a very sympathetic-sounding "Eeep?" and began to climb my leg.

"Oh, leave me alone," I said irritably.

"Turn not from solace when solace is offered," said the Tar. "The cup of pain cannot always be shared."

I sighed, but bent and let the chibling climb onto my shoulders. If it was going to insist on latching on to me, carrying it would be easier than walking with it wrapped around my leg.

Galuspa and his gang led us through the village. People watched curiously as we walked by, but no one said anything. We came at last to a house on the far side of town. Like all the other houses we had seen, it was circular, with round windows. (I hadn't seen a corner since we got here.) The mushroom-cap roof was brownish-orange, with splotches of deep forest green.

"You will stay here until the Ting Wongovia is ready to see you," said Galuspa. "Food will be brought to you." He paused, then added, "I hope you prove to be true friends. Though I have not known you long, I *do* like you. I will be happier if we can work together than if I have to dispose of you."

With that he opened the door and motioned for us to enter. I thought about asking him just what he meant by "dispose of us" but decided that I didn't really want to know.

We entered the house.

The door clicked shut behind us.

CHAPTER
13

The Tar's Offer

"WELL," SAID GRAKKER, TURNING TO MADAME PONG. "What do you suggest we do now?"

"Wait," she said serenely.

Grakker growled. Waiting was not his style.

"I suspect that is the best counsel, my captain," said Tar Gibbons. "With time, these people may yet be allies."

Grakker nodded. Then he turned and walked away from us. With a scream of rage he began smashing his head against the wall.

Tar Gibbons must have seen the look of horror on my face, for it extended its neck and rested its head on my shoulder. "Do not worry," it whispered. "The captain simply needs to get this out of his system. His head is *very* hard. It can stand the abuse with no trouble."

Indeed, though the wall had several deep dents when Grakker turned around, the captain himself looked much calmer, and none the worse for the wear.

"All right," he said. "We'll wait."

Which is exactly what we did.

For days and days and days.

The first night was fairly easy. With just a bit of exploration we found an underground floor with many small rooms clearly intended for sleeping—enough for each of us to have one to ourselves. I was so exhausted that when I lay down in the nestlike thing that I assumed was the shapeshifters' version of a bed, I fell asleep almost instantly (despite the fact that the chibling had wrapped itself around my feet).

The next morning was more difficult. Though it was a great relief to be able to rest and relax, it was hard to do so while waiting to be judged by the Ting Wongovia.

Moreover, when we had been traveling and in constant danger, I had been able to put aside thoughts of home. Now that we were standing still, they came crowding in on me.

"What do you suppose this Ting Wongovia is, anyway?" I asked when we gathered for breakfast.

Madame Pong made a gesture of uncertainty. "He, or she—"

"Or it," interrupted Tar Gibbons.

Madame Pong nodded. "Or *it* could be any of a number of things. Possibly a warlord. Possibly the village magician or wise man. Maybe a religious leader."

I blinked. It had never occurred to me that the Dimension X'ers would have religions. When I asked about this Madame Pong said, "The need for spiritual belief appears to be almost universal. In our own dimension, we are aware of only two planets in the civilized galaxy that lack some system for dealing with matters of the spirit. The variety of forms this takes is astonishing. But we find it nearly everywhere we go."

"Warrior Science calls for balance," said Tar Gibbons, shoveling a wad of *kispa-dinka* into its mouth. "Tend the body, tend the mind, tend the spirit."

"Do you think it will be hard to convince this Ting Wongovia that we really are on the same side?" I asked.

Madame Pong shrugged. "That is hard to say. It depends partly upon how suspicious these beings are. But such convincing is my job, and I think I do it fairly well."

Breakfast was actually fairly pleasant. It was the first chance we had all had to relax together, and it was a good opportunity for Elspeth to get to know a little more about the aliens. I fed the chibling wads of *kispa-dinka* while Elspeth asked her questions. She didn't seem too surprised by any of the answers until Tar Gibbons explained why it preferred to be called "it" rather than "he" or "she." (The short version is that "he" and "she" simply aren't sufficient to describe the variety of beings on the Tar's home planet.)

I had some questions of my own, such as "How did you find out that we had been brought to Dimension X?"

"Smorkus Flinders left plenty of clues," said Madame Pong.

Elspeth, always ready to point out someone else's flaws, said, "That was pretty careless of him."

"Not at all,' replied Tar Gibbons. "What is the point in setting a trap if you hide the bait so well that your quarry cannot find it?"

"You knew you were heading into a trap?" I exclaimed.

"Of course," said Grakker.

It is hard to tell you what it meant to me that the aliens knew this and came for me anyway. At that moment I felt I would do anything for the crew of the *Ferkel.*

"What happened to BKR?" I asked. "Were you able to take him to prison before you had to come after me?"

"We passed him off to one of the *Ferkel*'s sister ships," said Grakker. "The *Merkel* will have to complete that part of our mission."

I could tell by the sound of his voice that he did not like having someone else finish the job that he had started.

After breakfast we began to feel somewhat restless.

"How long do you suppose it will be before the Ting Wongovia summons us?" I asked.

Madame Pong's answer was interrupted by a short Reality Quake, during which I turned into a bug. Fortunately it was not one of the ones that left a permanent effect—though I did sort of like the fact that the walls of our prison had briefly disappeared. Unfortunately, it's hard to think of things like escaping when you're in the middle of a Reality Quake, and by the time any of us were capable of moving, the quake was over and the walls were back.

"I hate those things," said Elspeth. She seemed so shaken up that I decided not to tell her what *she* had looked like when it was going on. (I still haven't told her, so I can't write it down here. But if you think in terms of big ears, long floppy nose, and polka dots, you'll be on the right track.)

We had been too tired to explore the house completely the night before. Now we began to look around. It was Elspeth who found a door that opened onto a spiral ramp leading to the next floor. I thought the surface of the ramp was carpeted until I realized that it actually had some sort of plant life growing on it. It was very pleasant to walk on.

At the top of the ramp was an open space— pretty much the attic, I guess, except that it didn't have a ton of junk stored in it like every other attic I had ever seen. The space was round, with a gently arcing ceiling that started about five feet above floor level at the sides and soared to a good fifteen feet above us in the center of the space. This ceiling was the inside surface of one of the mushroomlike treetops that the shapeshifters used for roofs. It was translucent, so that the room was filled with a pleasant golden-brown light.

"Excellent," said Grakker. "We can exercise here."

I groaned. I *hate* exercise.

"Something the matter, Deputy Allbright?" asked Grakker fiercely.

"No, sir."

"I don't want to exercise," said Elspeth.

"*You* don't have to," replied Grakker. "You are not a deputy of the Galactic Patrol. However, the rest of us must keep ourselves fit for service."

"I want to be a deputy, too!" said Elspeth immediately. She hated being kept out of anything, even if it was something she didn't like.

Grakker rolled his eyes. "I will consider the matter."

"I want to be a deputy *now!*"

"I said I will consider the matter!" barked Grakker.

To my astonishment, Elspeth shut up. I don't think I had ever seen her do that for her parents, no matter how harshly they spoke to her. I was impressed. Obviously Grakker was born to command.

We exercised that morning, and again that afternoon. The chibling ran around making sounds of distress for a while, then settled itself next to me and tried to imitate my movements.

I was somewhat surprised when Madame Pong joined us—not because she was a woman, but because as ship's diplomat I thought she might be excused from such things. Elspeth exercised, too. I assume this was because she wanted to prove that she was fit to be a deputy, but it might have been out of sheer boredom. Even Phil worked out with us, though in his case (as he explained later) he did not exercise for strength— which for him depended entirely on nutrition and growth—but for flexibility.

Tar Gibbons also worked with us for part of each session, even leading some of the exercises. But then it would go off to do a separate program of its own. I assumed this was because a being with four legs and a neck as long as its arms has different exercise needs than your basic biped.

As before, I noticed that the Tar seemed to be paying an unusual amount of attention to me. It was beginning to make me nervous.

I finally found out what this was all about when the Tar came to me after dinner on our third night in the little house and said, "I have been watching you, Rod, and I would like to make you an offer."

"What kind of an offer?" I asked. I was exhausted from all the exercising, so I wasn't as enthusiastic as I might normally have been.

The Tar stretched its long neck so that its enormous eyes were level with mine. "If you will pledge yourself to me, I will teach you Warrior Science. Think before you answer!" it said, raising a hand to prevent me from speaking. "This will require a solemn vow. In the time that you are pledged to me, you will be my *krevlik*, which is to say that I will be your absolute master. I will teach you many secrets. I will help you train your body, and even more your mind, to do remarkable things. But you must pledge me your absolute obedience until your training is over. There is no other way."

CHAPTER
14

Katsu Maranda

I STARED AT THE TAR IN ASTONISHMENT. THOUGH IT is embarrassing to admit, my first thought was: *Cool! If I learn Warrior Science, I'll never have to worry about getting beat up on the playground again.*

Then I remembered that unless we could get out of this mess, I would never see the playground again.

"Do not answer now," said the Tar. "Sleep on it. You can give me your answer tomorrow."

Since I spent most of the night tossing and turning, I had a hard time following the Tar's advice to "sleep on it." But the offer was so exciting I couldn't settle down.

Remember, I had spent my entire life to that point as a clumsy, slightly overweight kid whose nickname was "Rod the Clod." While Tar Gibbons did not have a nickname, the "Tar" part of its name was actually an honorific, something like doctor or reverend or professor. In this case the title meant, roughly, "Wise and beloved warrior who can kill me with his little finger if he should so desire."

That was who wanted *me* for an apprentice!

I was torn between excitement at what the Tar could teach me and fear that I might let it down. Plus there was the requirement that I pledge my absolute obedience. What if the Tar told me something awful, like that I couldn't go home?

The chibling paced up and down beside my mattress, letting out an occasional *eeep*. I felt like *eeep*ing myself.

Here's how confused I was: I finally decided to go wake up Elspeth to talk to her about it. All right, all right, I know—but I had to talk to *someone*, and at the moment I needed someone human. Elspeth was the closest thing at hand.

With the chibling lolloping along beside me, I made my way down the dimly lit hall to her room, where I found her curled up in her nest.

"Wake up," I whispered, shaking her shoulder.

She snorted a little and made some cranky noises.

"Wake up!" I repeated.

Slowly she opened her eyes. "Rod!" she said groggily. "What are you doing here?"

"I have to talk to you."

To my surprise she sat up quickly, almost instantly alert. "About what?"

"Tar Gibbons has asked if I want to be its apprentice."

"So?"

"So I don't know what to do."

"Are you kidding?" said Elspeth. "Say yes! No offense, but this is probably the best chance you've got to stop being a pudgy clod."

"Thanks a lot."

She paused. "I'm sorry," she said, which startled me almost as much as the Tar's offer. "I know I shouldn't do that. I just can't help myself sometimes." She paused, then added, "I learned it from my mother."

I thought about that for a second, then realized that I had never heard Aunt Grace say anything nice to or about Elspeth. I had always figured it was because Elspeth was so rotten. Suddenly I wondered if maybe it was the other way around—if Elspeth was such a creep because of the way her parents treated her.

"It's all right," I said, sort of amazed at myself. "But do you really think I should do it? Before you answer, let me tell you the rest of it. I have to promise to do whatever the Tar tells me."

Elspeth paused. "Well, do you think it's going to make you eat horse manure or anything like that?" she asked at last.

"No. But what if it tells me I can't go home?"

She paused again, then said, "Why don't you ask if it's going to do that?"

I blinked. It had never occurred to me that I could ask something like that in advance.

"What if it won't tell me?"

"Then you'll have to think about it again," replied Elspeth. "But until you know, there's no sense in fussing about it."

I suppose you could say the point in fussing about it was to be prepared in case the Tar *did* say it was going to forbid me to go home (or refuse to tell me whether it might give that order). On the other hand, that could turn out to be a lot of fussing for nothing. Since I would be able to ask the Tar itself in just a few hours, Elspeth was right; there was no point in worrying about the matter until I knew for sure.

"Thanks," I said. I started to go. But she reached out her hand to stop me.

"Rod," she whispered urgently. "Do you think we'll ever get home?"

I paused. Though I had finally learned to lie as a result of my last adventure with the aliens, it was still hard for me. I looked at her carefully. Her eyes were pleading.

"Yes," I whispered, lying through my teeth. "I'm sure we will."

*   *   *

The next morning I went to Tar Gibbons and said, "I've been thinking about the offer you made me yesterday. I want to ask you a question."

The Tar nodded, but didn't say anything.

"Look, you wouldn't tell me that I couldn't go home or anything like that, would you?"

"I might."

I felt as if I had been hit in the stomach. During the night I had convinced myself that the Tar would just laugh and say, "Of course not." Now I was right back where I had started.

I took a deep breath. I started to ask if it was joking, realized by the look on its face that it wasn't, realized that I didn't know enough about the aliens to safely judge anything by their facial expressions, and finally blurted out, "You're *kidding!*"

The Tar shook its head regretfully. "No, I am quite serious. What is the point in pledging your obedience if you do so in the knowledge that you're not going to have to do something you don't want to do? Warrior Science does not allow for those who do things with half a heart. Either you are my krevlik or you are not. If you are, then you must take on the task with every ounce of courage and devotion that you possess."

"I'll get back to you," I whispered.

I watched the Tar carefully during our exercise sessions that day. It moved with amazing grace and precision. I remembered our battle with BKR, when the Tar had managed to knock our enemy to the floor, even though the Tar itself was only two inches high at the time.

My father was gone. Who would teach me to be a man?

That evening I went to the Tar and said, "I wish to be your krevlik."

It nodded solemnly. "Follow me."

We went to the mushroom attic, where we performed a ceremony that I may not tell you about and I pledged my obedience to my master, my teacher, Tar Gibbons.

When we were done, the Tar said, "Welcome to the Brotherhood of Warriors. With me you will learn to fight, with the hope that you will never have to fight. You will turn your body into a lethal weapon, with the prayer that you will never have to use it. You will seek Katsu Maranda, with the goal of passing it on to all those you meet."

"Katsu Maranda?"

"It is the secret of the Cheerful Warrior," said the Tar. "It means 'To be in Joyful Harmony with the universe.' This is the source of your greatest strength. It is the fountain from which your spirit will drink. It will make you a rock, a lightning bolt, a star."

The Tar turned. "Follow me," it said.

I followed it down the stair.

The others were gathered in the living room. I wondered if the Tar was going to announce that I had become its krevlik. It cleared its throat and started to speak but a sharp knocking at the door interrupted.

The Tar glanced at me. I went to answer.

Before I could reach the door, it swung open by itself and in stepped Galuspa (or some shape-shifter who had decided to look like Galuspa). He looked at us, then said, "The Ting Wongovia will see you now."

CHAPTER
15

The Ting Wongovia

MADAME PONG SCURRIED BEHIND GRAKKER AND DID a quick module change. "Diplomatic module," she whispered when she saw me watching her. "Doesn't work very well, but it may keep him from ruining the situation entirely."

With Grakker in the lead, we marched out of the house, chibling and all. A dozen shapeshifters armed with ray guns stood ready to keep us in line.

They marched us through the center of the village. On the far side we stopped in front of a house no bigger or fancier than the one in which we were being held. Standing in front of the door, Galuspa said, "This is the home of the Ting Wongovia. In his decision lies your fate."

With those cheerful words, he opened the door and gestured for us to enter.

One by one we filed through the door into a

dark room. At the far side hung a shimmering blue-black curtain, covered with stars and moons that drifted in slowly changing patterns.

Once we were all inside, the door closed silently behind us, leaving us in complete darkness save for the slight glow of the patterns of the curtain. This darkness lasted only a moment.

Then the curtain was drawn aside to reveal the Ting Wongovia.

He sat in an ornately carved chair, bathed in a column of blue light. He wore a robe of the same shimmering blue-black fabric as the curtain. And his face was so familiar it made me gasp in astonishment.

My gasp was nothing compared to Grakker's shout of joy.

While my astonishment lasted, the captain's joy, alas, did not. The being facing us was not, as we had first thought, our missing friend Flinge Iblik. He merely looked enough like our lost crew member to be his brother.

After gazing at us solemnly for what seemed like several minutes, he said, "Greetings. As you have no doubt guessed, I am the current Ting Wongovia. My apologies that I was not able to see you sooner. I was . . . otherwise engaged."

"Where is Flinge Iblik?" shouted Grakker.

The lizard-faced being sitting in the chair looked as surprised as I had felt when we first saw him. "What do you know of Flinge Iblik?" he asked sharply.

Madame Pong moved up beside Grakker and put a hand on his arm to remind him that such conversations were her job. "Flinge Iblik is our shipmate," she said.

"And he is my egg-brother," replied the Ting Wongovia, "which in many ways is almost the same thing. But if he is your shipmate, why is he not with you? Why do you ask if *I* know where he is?"

Quickly Madame Pong told the story of Snout's disappearance. As she spoke, the Ting Wongovia began to frown. "This is not good," he said when she was done. "Not good at all—especially in light of what else is going on."

"What else *is* going on?" asked Madame Pong. The way she asked the question made me shudder, for it gave me the feeling that we had stumbled into a bigger problem than I had realized; that we were not simply fighting for our own survival but facing something bigger, something we did not yet understand.

The Ting Wongovia did not answer her question, at least not directly. "I need to examine you before I say more," he replied. "I do not yet know that you are safe, or that I would be wise in trusting you."

"What do you propose?" asked Madame Pong.

"If you truly knew Flinge Iblik, then you already know the answer to that."

"You want to do a mind probe," said Madame Pong.

"I forbid it!" snapped Grakker.

The Ting Wongovia looked at him in surprise. "How else am I to know whether I can trust you?"

"How do I know that we can trust *you?*" retorted Grakker.

The Ting Wongovia smiled. "You don't."

"I can well believe that you are Flinge Iblik's egg-brother," snarled Grakker. "That's exactly the kind of answer I used to get from *him*. Even so, I am not going to allow you to look into the mind of any of my crew. To do so would give you access to information you could use to destroy us. And just as you cannot be certain that we are on your side against Smorkus Flinders, we cannot be certain what your motives are."

"Alas," said the Ting Wongovia, "it seems we are at an impasse. Your concerns are valid. Yet until I am sure that your good will is equally so, I cannot let you join us. We simply have too much at stake."

"What we need," said Madame Pong, "is someone whose mind will reflect our good faith, yet does not hold our secrets."

"Precisely," said the Ting Wongovia.

You can probably see where this was heading.

I didn't, until Madame Pong said, "Deputy All-bright, would you step forward?"

I swallowed hard. Though I didn't particularly want this guy rummaging around inside my head, I could see why I was the one who was going to have to volunteer. A probe of my mind would certainly show that the crew of the *Ferkel* was not working for Smorkus Flinders. However, unless the Ting Wongovia had a burning desire to know the details of life as a sixth grader in a small town on Earth, his probe was not likely to turn up anything else of interest.

"Go on, Roddie," hissed Elspeth. "They're waiting for you!"

This annoyed me so much that I wanted to stay where I was just to spite her. But there was too much at stake. Taking a deep breath, I stepped up beside Madame Pong and Grakker and said, "Deputy Allbright reporting for duty."

"I shall have to ask the rest of you to leave us," said the Ting Wongovia.

Grakker started to protest, but the Ting Wongovia raised his right hand and said, "I will be very vulnerable while conducting the probe. I cannot have potential enemies in the room while I am doing so. You will return to your quarters now. When I am done with your deputy, we will talk again."

Though Grakker grumbled, Madame Pong made a gesture of assent. The aliens turned to go.

"What are you doing?" cried Elspeth. "You can't just leave Rod here with that guy! There's no telling what he might do to him."

I was startled by this display of loyalty from Elspeth. Unfortunately, it didn't have much effect other than to crank up my fear and uncertainty.

Madame Pong turned toward me. "Do you accept this assignment, Deputy Allbright?"

"Of course he does," growled Grakker.

"Captain!" she said sharply. "You know that Provision 136.9.17.48 of the Galactic Code forbids us to force anyone to undergo a mind probe. Since the question has arisen, we must again determine that Deputy Allbright is doing this of his own free will." She turned to me and said, "Deputy Allbright?"

I hesitated. This was my chance out of it. The truth was, I was terrified by the thought of the Ting Wongovia poking around inside my brain. But if I refused, what then? We would be right back where we started.

I glanced at the Tar, wondering if it would order me to volunteer. Even if Grakker couldn't order me to do this, the Tar could, now that I was its krevlik. But its face was a blank.

The decision was mine alone.

"Is this mind probe thing dangerous?" I asked.

"Not really," said the Ting Wongovia. "There is a small chance that you will be driven completely mad by the process. But the odds of that happening are really quite low."

"How low?"

The Ting Wongovia smiled. "Exactly equal to the chance that it will happen to me instead."

I sighed. For a minute I thought I had a good excuse to bow out. But if the Ting Wongovia was willing to take the chance, I couldn't refuse without looking like a total coward. One of Mom's lectures started playing in the back of my head— the one about not worrying about what other people think of me, and just doing what is right.

Okay, so if it didn't matter if the others thought I was a coward I could still bow out if I wanted to.

But would it be right?

I sighed. "All right, I'll do it."

Grakker smiled.

The aliens tried to take the chibling with them when they left, but it *eeep*ed so desperately that finally the Ting Wongovia gestured for them to leave it behind.

"Bye, Roddie," called Elspeth as the door closed behind them. "Good luck!"

She actually sounded like she meant it.

I was alone with the Ting Wongovia.

He chuckled and rubbed his hands together.

"Well," he said with a smile that I could not interpret. "This ought to be interesting."

CHAPTER
16

Bubble Memories

THE ALIEN SAID NOTHING ELSE FOR THE NEXT SEVERAL minutes, just stared at me in silence. I wondered if he was trying to get into my mind; if he was, I sure didn't feel it. Finally, moving slowly, he touched a button on his chair. The blue light disappeared. Only then did I realize that the light had probably been a force field protecting him from possible attack. I stifled a snort. I was so used to getting beat up that it was hard to believe someone could actually consider *me* a threat.

Leaning forward, the Ting Wongovia said, "How well did you know my egg-brother?"

"Not very. Flinge Iblik and I went through a dangerous time together a while ago. I learned great respect for him. But I don't really know much about him."

"You will know more about him, or at least about our people, when this experience is over," said the Ting Wongovia. "You see, it is impossible for me to do a mind probe without opening myself to you at the same time. Not completely, of course; I am, after all, a Master of the Mental Arts. And unless you have had more experience with this than I suspect, you will not know how to take advantage of the situation. Even so, you will inevitably learn much about me—and, by extension, much about my egg-brother. Are you ready to begin?"

I took a deep breath. "Yes," I whispered. "I'm ready."

The Ting Wongovia rose from his chair and walked to where I stood. Placing his spindly fingers at my temples, he raised his face toward mine.

The chibling let out a shriek and wrapped itself around my leg. This made me nervous. Did the little creature know something that I didn't? I half expected the Ting Wongovia to order me to do something about the animal, but he simply gave it a quick glance then returned his attention to me, as if the chibling's presence was a matter of no importance.

The stance he had taken was familiar—it was the same one Snout had used when he did the "training transfer" that taught me how to use the flying belt. Except that time Snout and I had been the same height, because we had both been shrunk to about two inches. At our regular sizes, the head of his egg-brother came only slightly above my waist.

"You probably don't want me to move," I said, remembering how disastrous it had been when I broke my connection to Snout.

"Don't worry about it," replied the Ting Wongovia. "You won't be able to."

Naturally, I responded to this statement by trying to move. The Ting Wongovia had spoken the truth: I was completely immobilized.

"This will be easier if you relax," he said.

There it is again, I thought. *Stay calm.* The advice was turning out to have more uses than I would have guessed.

While I was wondering again how much I had missed by not reading further in Flinge Iblik's book, I found myself beginning to drift. . . .

Suddenly I was no longer just myself, but (somehow) both myself and the Ting Wongovia.

I felt as if I were suspended in some strange sea. Around me floated memories, drifting up like bubbles of a thousand colors, a thousand sizes. Every once in a while one of the bubbles would burst against me and flood me with its contents: experiences so vivid and clear it was as if they were my own, as if I had *become* the Ting Wongovia, and was not merely remembering but actually living the incidents contained in each bubble.

*　　　*　　　*

Bubble: I am hatching—breaking my way out of my leathery egg and stretching into the sunshine. Around me squeak and wiggle my egg-brothers and egg-sisters, all three hundred and fifty-eight of them. Our voices rise in the hatching song.

Bubble: I am entering a beautiful wooden building. My long face twitches with nervousness. Yet I am happy, proud because out of all my egg-brothers and egg-sisters only Flinge Iblik and myself have been chosen to be trained in the Mental Arts. One other from our hatching year, a female named Selima Khan, has also been selected. Together we have traveled across space to the Mentat. Today our training is to begin.

Bubble: I am buried beneath a writhing mass of furry bodies, trying to squirm my way free.

(Later I realized that this bubble—and this bubble only—came not from the Ting Wongovia, but was some vague memory of the chibling's that got mixed in with the whole situation!)

Bubble: A being who looks like a three-legged avocado with tentacles takes my face between its hands and begins to weep.

Bubble: Seething with rage and frustration, I throw my few belongings into a sack and climb out a window.

Bubble: I stand in darkness, listening not with my ears but with my mind. At first I have a hard

time picking out the speakers, but soon I am able to separate their voices. It takes only a moment for me to feel a wave of horror at what they are saying. I start to move. . . .

I felt as if I had been shaken out of an intense dream. The memory-remnants of the last bubble spattered about inside my brain, leaving mysterious and unconnected images. It was as if I had been watching a movie and someone had ripped the last reel off the projector, cut the film into tiny pieces, and dumped them into my hand saying, "Here, figure out the rest of the story yourself!"

The chibling flopped off my leg and lay there *eeep*ing weakly.

The Ting Wongovia was staring at me with an expression that I could not interpret. Finally he said, "That was made much easier by your previous experience with my egg-brother. Allow me to say that you have a very interesting mind, Rod Allbright."

"Do you trust us now?" I asked eagerly.

He made a sign of acceptance. "Unless the rest of your crew is operating at a deep level of deceit, you are what you say you are."

The words made me shiver. Was it possible Grakker and the others were something different than they had told me, on some other mission than they claimed to be? I shook away the idea. Grakker was too straightforward for that kind of thing. But what about Madame Pong? Her mind was sly and subtle. She could work at many levels. . . .

Stop it! I told myself angrily.

The Ting Wongovia was smiling at me. "I have summoned the others," he said. "Now that I am satisfied with your intentions, we can talk. I think you will find this . . . *interesting.*"

Something about the way he said "interesting" made me shiver again.

In about ten minutes the other aliens (I say "other aliens" because by this time I had realized that in Dimension X I was an alien as well) came through the door. Galuspa was with them.

Elspeth looked intently into my eyes. "Did you go crazy?" she asked, giving me a ghoulish grin.

"You'll never know," I whispered. "At least, not until it's too late!"

Then I let out a low but demented laugh.

The look on her face was very satisfactory.

Madame Pong paused beside me. "You have done well, Rod," she said. "You have my thanks. And the captain will enter this in your record. Since you also got a commendation for your help in the struggle against BKR, this will look very good for you. My congratulations."

"You keep a record on me?" I asked in surprise.

She seemed surprised at my surprise. "You are a deputy of the Galactic Patrol," she said. "Of course we keep a record on you."

Though Grakker had always called me a deputy, I had figured it was just a way for him to justify bossing me around. But if they were keeping a record on me, it must mean I really *was* a member of the Galactic Patrol!

I felt as if I had just learned that I had accidentally joined the army.

I was still trying to figure out what all this meant when my thoughts were interrupted by the Ting Wongovia.

"Please make yourselves comfortable," he said. "There is much that we must discuss. What I have learned from your deputy tells me that things are worse—much worse—than I had realized."

CHAPTER
17

Unite and Conquer

THE TING WONGOVIA'S WORDS CREATED AN UNEASY murmur.

"Please, please," he said, holding up his hands. "Find a seat. Settle in. This is going to take some time."

The lights came up so that the room was merely dim instead of dark. I couldn't figure out who had adjusted them, then decided that either the Ting Wongovia had a switch in his chair or had somehow done it with his mind.

In the murky light I could see a variety of chairs and cushions against the curving wall. Each of us quickly found something suitable, with the exception of Galuspa, who simply turned himself into a legless blob. The chibling stretched itself out at my feet.

"All right," growled Grakker, once we were all seated. "What 'things' are you talking about?"

"The fate of Rod's planet," said the Ting Wongovia. "And, by extension, the fate of our entire dimension, which is in immediate and terrible danger."

When the Ting Wongovia said "our" dimension, it took me a moment to remember that he had not been born in Dimension X, but was a visitor here like the rest of us. I wondered how he had ended up here, in this village, in this role.

If only I had been able to make more use of that mind probe!

"What did you find in Rod's memories that indicated this danger?" asked Madame Pong.

"The image of Smorkus Flinders moving between the dimensions. He did it *far* too easily. I know you are well aware of what a complicated thing it is to breach the dimensional barriers. Yet Smorkus Flinders went in and out of our dimension as if he were stepping through a door. That means his research has finally paid off."

"Research?" I asked.

Madame Pong shot me a look, reminding me that as ship's diplomat, this conversation was in her hands.

The Ting Wongovia answered anyway. "Smorkus Flinders has one of the greatest minds ever seen on this planet. He was also quite a nice person, until he got turned into a monster. Then everything changed."

"Turned into a monster?" asked Madame Pong.

"I see I need to fill you in on life in this part of Dimension X," said the Ting Wongovia. "Aside from minor species like the chiblings, there are three types of sentient life here—the normals, the shapeshifters, and the monsters. The normals are not unlike most of the intelligent species in our own dimension. However, they are subject to something we in Dimension Q are not, namely Reality Quakes. Most of the quakes are frightening but relatively harmless. Under certain circumstances, though, their effects are permanent. Every once in a while one of the normals is caught in a Reality Quake and changed forever. When Smorkus Flinders was slightly beyond Rod's level of maturity he was caught in the worst Reality Quake in living memory. It changed him from a fun-loving young man to the monstrosity that you know.

"Like everyone so afflicted Smorkus Flinders was forced to leave his village and move to the Valley of the Monsters, a section of the planet set aside for the quake-victims. There he continued to grow. By the time he became a full adult his size had made him the complete master of that domain.

"Unfortunately, the experience had changed him inside as well as outside. Bitter and angry at his transformation and the loss of his love partner, he turned his great intelligence toward destructive ends. For many years now he has been the scourge of this planet. His wrath has been directed especially toward the shapeshifters; he is jealous of them because they are immune to the Reality Quakes."

I glanced at Galuspa.

"An evolutionary response," he said, stretching out a pair of shoulders so that he could shrug. "If you can change your shape at will, a Reality Quake doesn't make that much difference to you."

"Smorkus Flinders resented this immunity," continued the Ting Wongovia. "And resented, too, knowing that in other dimensions Reality Quakes do not occur at all. I have a spy in Castle Chaos who informs me that for years Smorkus Flinders has been seeking a simple way to cross between the dimensions. It seemed like a pointless quest—no one thought he would ever succeed. Now that he has, the consequences may be horrendous."

"Why is that?" asked Madame Pong.

"Because my spy informs me that our enemy has in mind a plan that will basically end life as we know it, not only on Earth, but possibly across *all* of Dimension Q. To put it bluntly, our entire universe is in peril."

Everyone shifted uneasily. I felt a knot of tension growing in my stomach, fear for my mother and the Things, for Aunt Grace and Uncle Roger, for Mickey and my friends—even for my father, wherever he was.

"And this plan is?" prompted Madame Pong.

The Ting Wongovia stood for the first time. "Smorkus Flinders wants to create a permanent opening between the two dimensions. If I am reading the signs correctly, this opening will be located in the field behind Rod's house."

The knot in my stomach grew tighter.

"You see it was no accident that BKR was living in Rod's town," continued the Ting Wongovia. "He and Smorkus Flinders were working together to create this gap between the dimensions, and I suspect that Smorkus Flinders's research had shown him that the most likely place to make the bridge is in the place that Rod calls Seldom Seen. Nor is it an accident that this spot was on Rod's planet. Earth is one of the major nexus points for the two dimensions, one of the places where they are most closely linked, and the barriers are weakest."

Turning to me, the Ting Wongovia said, "It is probable that Earth's proximity to Dimension X, where Reality Quakes are such a problem, is one reason the people on your planet have such a slim grasp on reality. I suspect there is some kind of vibrational overlap that makes you all slightly crazy."

"That would explain a lot," I murmured, trying to figure out whether the entire human race had just been insulted, or excused for its bad behavior.

"Anyway," continued the Ting Wongovia. "The immediate danger is to Rod's planet. If Smorkus Flinders does manage to make a permanent opening the Reality Quakes will almost certainly leak over to Earth. Given the current state of the planet's mental health, it is likely that everyone there will quickly go quite mad."

Not to mention occasionally turning into monsters, I thought.

"But that is not the end of the danger. As you know, dimensions occupy the same space, but in different vibrational planes. Once the gate is opened, the convergence will spread, slowly at first but ever faster, until the two dimensions are completely meshed into a single universe where reality can shift like sand."

"Why would anyone do something that horrible?" cried Elspeth.

The Ting Wongovia spread his hands. "For Smorkus Flinders, who is half mad, it is a kind of revenge, a way of lashing out at life for what it did to him. As for BKR—alas, I cannot begin to understand his motives."

"Pure nastiness," said Grakker. "Even the fact that this will affect him as much as anyone else doesn't matter. He doesn't care what happens to him, as long as he is causing pain to others."

I remembered Madame Pong's words when she was describing BKR's cruelty: *"Millions have wept."* I shivered. If this new plan succeeded, the number of those who wept would not be in the millions; it would be beyond counting.

"We have to stop Smorkus Flinders," said Grakker.

"Clearly," said the Ting Wongovia. "The question is: *How?* The shapeshifters have been trying for years, but he is too powerful for them."

"What about the normals?" asked Madame Pong.

The Ting Wongovia shook his head. "Completely subdued."

"I shall arrest him in the name of the Galactic Patrol," said Grakker.

That's what I liked best about the captain. He was so straightforward.

The Ting Wongovia smiled gently. "Excellent suggestion, Captain Grakker. But the question remains: How?"

Grakker scowled. "Help us get back to the monster's castle. If we can regain our ship, we may be able to subdue him."

The Ting Wongovia raised an eyebrow. "You would put yourselves back in his grasp? From what I saw in Rod's mind, he seems to have a special anger toward you, in particular, Captain. His vengeance if he catches you will be terrible indeed. Can you tell me why that is, by the way?"

"That is classified information," said Grakker, putting on his stubborn face.

The Ting Wongovia nodded. "As you will. However, I would still like you to explain what good it will do you to regain your ship."

Grakker scowled, and I could tell he was trying to decide whether or not to trust the Ting Wongovia. Finally he answered the question with a question. "What are you doing here? Why aren't you in Dimension Q where you belong?"

The Ting Wongovia smiled. "That is classified information," he said gently.

Grakker's scowl deepened. Madame Pong stepped in. "Our first step would probably be to return to Dimension Q for reinforcements."

The Ting Wongovia shook his head. "I'm not sure that is a good idea. Though my spy's reports lead me to think that Smorkus Flinders has reasons for waiting, should you escape I suspect that he will put his plans into motion immediately. The wound between the dimensions would likely be beyond repair before you could find help."

Madame Pong remained calm. "Then we can attempt to shrink the monster," she said.

"Unlikely," replied the Ting Wongovia. "He will almost certainly be shielded against it."

"Couldn't we enlarge ourselves instead?" I

asked, forgetting that I was supposed to remain silent.

"Not really a good idea," said Phil.

"Why not? You're always shrinking and enlarging the ship, not to mention everyone in it."

"Yes, but all those enlargements really do is return us to our normal size," replied the plant. "What you are suggesting is that we actually make someone bigger than they are designed to be. That sort of enlarging is a much more complicated prospect than shrinking someone, and somewhat dangerous. It stretches a being past what is good for it."

"I can handle it," said Tar Gibbons calmly. "If need be, we can enlarge me."

"That may be our only option," said the Ting Wongovia.

CHAPTER
18

Warrior Training

"WHAT IS THE ENEMY?" ASKED TAR GIBBONS.

"Sloth," I replied, stretching to the right.

"What is the enemy?" it repeated.

"Fear," I said, stretching to the left.

The Tar and I were standing on a hill outside the village of the shapeshifters, in the dim light of a very early morning. The little red plants were just beginning to sing. It was two weeks after our meeting with the Ting Wongovia (counting a week as seven periods of waking and sleeping, though I had no idea how long days and nights actually lasted here). After that meeting we had been given our freedom to go wherever we pleased, and this morning my teacher and I had come to the hilltop so that the Tar could drill me in the warrior's litany.

The chibling was standing beside me, imitating my movements. It was pretty funny, but after the first week I had trained myself to concentrate on what I was doing and ignore the little creature even when it was being cute.

"What is the enemy?" asked the Tar for the third time.

I stood straight and answered as calmly as I could.

"Anger."

My teacher nodded. "Very good. Each of these enemies will keep you from being all that you can be. If you are slothful, you will not keep your body tuned to be a precise fighting machine. This does not mean that you should not rest when appropriate. If you are fearful, you will not think clearly. This does not mean that you should not be wise and cautious. If you let anger rule you, you will not know when to fight and when not to. This does not mean that you should not use righteous anger to fuel your strength."

Then it began showing me a new series of stretching exercises. They hurt just a little, but I didn't mind, because even though it had only been two weeks since we started working, I was already starting to feel the effects.

In fact, between the stress of our adventure and the workouts and exercises I was doing with Tar Gibbons, I was not only getting stronger, I was actually getting rid of some of my pudge! And it was exciting to be learning how to use my body more effectively. I was sick to death of being known as Rod the Clod.

"What is the greatest source of strength?" asked the Tar.

"Joy!" I grunted, lunging forward and kicking sideways.

"Excellent. When it is time to fight, you must touch the joy that underlies the universe; take it in as if you were breathing it. When you are in joyful harmony with the universe, you will know what you are fighting for. Quick—down and sideways!"

And so it went. By the time we returned to the house for breakfast, my body was aching and sweat was streaming down my forehead. Yet I felt, to my own surprise, very happy.

When I mentioned this to the Tar, it said, "Of course you're happy. You're doing something real, something that challenges you. How else would you feel?"

"But it was hard work," I said.

The Tar's eyes got bigger than usual. "Do you associate work with unhappiness?" it asked in astonishment. Then, before I could answer, it said, "Never mind. Sometimes I forget where you come from."

"What's that supposed to mean?" I asked, offended on the planet's behalf.

The Tar spread its hands. "Most of your work

isn't real," it said. "Real work gives joy. False work breeds despair."

"Would you explain that please?"

"No. Think about it. It will be good for you."

I sighed. I got that kind of answer from the Tar a lot. Fortunately, it didn't do anything to dampen my good feelings. I was humming as we went back into the house.

Still, it was not easy to maintain that feeling all the time. It was only when Tar and I were working that I was able to forget my frustration at the fact that we were not yet moving against Smorkus Flinders.

I could understand the delay; we had a lot of planning to do if our mission was not to fail. And failure was something that we could not allow ourselves. But every day was an agony of waiting and worrying. If not for the distraction of training, I think I would have gone mad.

Grakker was pacing the floor when we returned from our practice session. I think he was even more frustrated than I was.

"The Ting Wongovia is the most annoying being I have ever had to work with!" he shouted when he saw us. "Closemouthed! Arrogant! Bossy!"

Since this was also a fair description of Grakker, I could see why the two of them would not get along very well.

Before we could respond, Galuspa burst into

146

the room, his eyes big, his legs stretched to running length. "The Ting Wongovia has just received word from his spy that Smorkus Flinders will soon make his move against Dimension Q. We must leave for the Valley of the Monsters today!"

That suited all of us just fine, with the exception of Elspeth, who had been assigned to stay behind in the village of the shapeshifters.

It had not been a pleasant conversation.

"I *won't* stay!" she had said. "If Rod can go, I can go!"

"Rod is a deputy of the Galactic Patrol," Madame Pong had explained. "He has no choice. You are a civilian and are to be spared such things."

"I can't believe you're doing this to me!" Elspeth shouted. "You're a woman! How will we ever be equal if we don't stick together?"

Madame Pong had looked puzzled for a moment. Then she smiled. "That is not an issue where I come from," she said gently. "In the civilized parts of the galaxy *all* intelligent beings are given equal rights and opportunities. The way women are treated on your planet is one of the things the rest of us find most puzzling about your world."

From the way she had said that, I got the feeling that our treatment of women was also one of the reasons Earth had not yet been invited to join the League of Worlds. I would have asked about it, but Madame Pong had long ago made it clear that our planet's exclusion from "the civilized galaxy" was something she would not discuss.

Her answer hadn't impressed Elspeth. "Are you telling me things are different with you guys?" she had asked. "Look at the *Ferkel*. *You're* the only woman on the crew!"

That comment had provoked one of the merriest laughs I ever heard from Madame Pong. "Do you actually presume to understand the civilized galaxy based on the crew of one ship?" she had replied incredulously. "We have millions of ships, Elspeth. Some have crews that are *all* male. Others have crews that are all female. Some have crews that are evenly divided between male and female. Others have crews in which at least sixteen different genders are represented. My dear Elspeth, anyone who assumes to know the whole on the basis of such a small sample will be wrong at least as often as they are right."

Elspeth had blinked, uncertain of how to respond to this statement. Finally she had crossed her arms and said, "It's not fair."

"Not much is," Madame Pong had replied.

We set out as darkness was falling. Somewhat to my surprise, the Ting Wongovia was traveling with us. Since I had not been in on the planning sessions, I hadn't known that he would be coming, and had pretty much assumed he was going to stay home and be wise or something.

We were also accompanied by a small army of shapeshifters, led by Galuspa. This was because to reach the castle where Smorkus Flinders lived, we were going to have to travel through monster territory and protection might be necessary. One cool thing about the shapeshifters was that they could work together; if we saw a monster coming early enough, they could do something like turn themselves into a small hill, with those of us who were unable to alter our shapes tucked safely inside. The idea was not to fight, but to get to the castle without anyone realizing that we were on our way.

Because the shapeshifters knew the best combination of transporter ovals to get us there quickly, the trip back to Smorkus Flinders's castle was shorter than I had expected.

"Not that we're traveling in a straight line," explained the Ting Wongovia, as we paused before one of the ovals. "This oval, for example, is going to take us to the far side of the planet. But it lets us off only a half day's walk from another oval that will drop us within a few feet of the Valley of the Monsters."

I swallowed hard. When I had thought that we were going to spend days getting back to the castle, it had seemed like we were starting out on a glorious adventure, with a long stretch before the real danger started. As it turned out, the danger would be close at hand almost immediately.

The section of the planet set aside for victims of Reality Quakes was not very pleasant. The ground in Monster Valley was rough and rocky, and a layer of *kispa-dinka* floated everywhere. The good thing about this was that it made it easier than I expected to hide from the monsters, since many of them were so tall that their heads were above the bottom level of the *kispa-dinka*. However, unlike Smorkus Flinders, who was so tall that his head reached well above the stuff many of the smaller monsters—those between three and eight times my height—were forced to walk around with their heads right *in* it. I figured this was not apt to make them good-natured.

Shortly after we entered the valley, we heard a commotion behind us. I turned around. To my dismay I saw Elspeth running toward us, shouting, "Wait for me! Wait for me!"

Two of the shapeshifters darted toward her, clapping their hands over her mouth as soon as they caught her.

"What are *you* doing here?" I hissed as they carried her into the center of our group.

She couldn't answer, of course, since the shapeshifters still had her mouth covered. When she finally stopped struggling, the Ting Wongovia motioned for them to let her speak.

"I followed you," she said. "And it wasn't easy. But you know your mother said you were supposed to keep an eye on me, Rod. You had no business going off and leaving me!"

"Silence!" said Grakker. "We will discipline you later, young woman."

"You're not the boss of me!" said Elspeth.

This was not a smart thing to say to Grakker. When he was done telling Elspeth exactly what he thought of her attitude, her antics, and her lack of discipline, even I felt sorry for her.

"We will proceed in silence," Grakker said at last. Pointing to a pair of the shapeshifters, he said, "Walk beside her and make sure she does not make any sounds that might betray us."

We started out again.

The castle loomed before us like some mountainous nightmare. But sneaking into it was not as difficult as I expected, for two reasons. First, a wall that seems tight and secure to someone as big as Smorkus Flinders can still have some pretty big holes in it. Second, the Ting Wongovia knew exactly where to find those holes.

Though we entered at what seemed like ground

level, we found ourselves sliding down a wall. Then I remembered how things shifted and slid in Castle Chaos.

With the Ting Wongovia leading the way, we pressed ourselves against the joint where the surface that was currently the floor met one of the walls. We scurried along like an army of mice, passing through one room, and then another, and still another. The current ceilings loomed far above us. The things that hung on the walls were stranger than I can explain, the sounds and smells beyond my ability to describe.

Twice we managed to remain unseen while monsters—servants of Smorkus Flinders, I assumed—lumbered past us.

The third time we were not so lucky. I can still remember the rush of fear I felt when we entered a large room and Spar Kellis stepped from a shadow to squat down in front of us.

"I thought you were never going to get here!" said the giant blue blob.

Then he started to drool.

CHAPTER
19

Krevlik's Duty

I FIGURED THIS WAS THE END. EITHER SPAR KELLIS would hand us over to his "glorious boss" Smorkus Flinders or simply squash us and eat us on the spot.

Or maybe he would skip the squashing part and just eat us alive.

Neither of these happened. Instead, the Ting Wongovia threw out his arms and said, "Thank goodness you're here! I was beginning to think I was leading us in the wrong direction." Turning to the rest of us, he said, "Allow me to present the spy that I have mentioned to you—my good and faithful friend Spar Kellis." Turning back to the monster he whispered, "Wipe your chin, Sparkles. You're drooling."

Looking embarrassed, Spar Kellis scrubbed the back of his hand over his chin. "Please excuse me," he said, glancing past the Ting Wongovia to the rest of us. "I can't help it."

"They understand," said the Ting Wongovia. "Now, can you get us to the ship?"

"All of you?" asked Spar Kellis uneasily.

"That would be best."

"All right, wait a minute."

He walked through one of the walls, then reappeared a few minutes later with a grubby sack about three times the size of a phone booth. "Climb in here," he said.

Grakker looked at the Ting Wongovia. "Are you sure we can trust him?"

The Ting Wongovia spread his hands. "I have put my life in his hands more than once. Beside, if we can't trust him we're doomed anyway, so what is there to lose?"

And with that he climbed into the sack.

Grakker hesitated, then motioned for the rest of us to follow. In we went: Tar Gibbons, Phil, Madame Pong, Elspeth, Grakker, Galuspa, the shapeshifters, the chibling, and me. It was smelly and dark inside, and when Spar Kellis picked up the bag, we all fell together in a jumble. The shapeshifters acted quickly to keep us from getting squashed; forming themselves into bars and arches, they stretched out the bag and lifted themselves away from those of us on the bottom. Once they did that it was still smelly and dark, but at least I could breathe.

The discomfort was worth it, because less than

five minutes later Spar Kellis set the bag down, opened the top, and whispered, "Here we are." Climbing out, we found ourselves standing on a table the size of a football field. About ten feet from us was possibly the most beautiful thing I have ever seen: the *Ferkel!*

"Ah," sighed Grakker. "My ship. Quickly, crew—inside, so that we can begin to repair the damages." Turning to Spar Kellis, he asked, "How much time do we have?"

"I can make no guarantees," said the huge blue monster, wiping away the stream of drool running over his chin. "While Smorkus Flinders does not come here often, there is nothing to guarantee he will *not* come."

Grakker nodded. "Thank you for your help."

"The only thanks I want is the defeat of Smorkus Flinders! Now I must go. If I am missing too long, he will grow suspicious. Be wise. Be brave. Fight well. We are all counting on you."

"We will do our best," said Grakker. Then he led the way into the ship.

The rest of the crew went with him, as did the Ting Wongovia.

The shapeshifters, however, flattened themselves out so that they looked like the surface of the table.

"Phil, assess the damages," ordered Grakker as soon as we were inside. "First check the enlarging and shrinking rays. Then make sure we are sealed tight. Finally check the mechanisms that will allow us to return to our own dimension. Madame Pong, help him as you are able. The rest of you go below and stay out of the way. Tar Gibbons, you are excused from other assignments so that you may prepare to fight."

"I wish to have my krevlik with me," said the Tar.

Grakker looked at me, then nodded. "As you will. After all, both law and custom dictate that if you should fall, your apprentice must take up the battle."

I couldn't tell if he was teasing or not.

I followed the Tar to its room, which I had seen briefly the last time I was on the ship. I hoped it wasn't going to make me wait there with it. Like each of the aliens, the Tar's room was designed to suit its specific needs and tastes. In this case that meant that the room was actually a pond with a single large rock in the center. A thick mist floated over the pond. High, squeaking sounds filled the air. I wasn't sure exactly what the little winged creatures that made them were called, only that the Tar used them for snacks and was apt to grab them out of the air as they went flying by.

We paused at the door. The Tar opened a small

panel and began to fiddle with some dials. To my surprise, a path rose from the pond's surface. It led not to the rock in the center of the room, but to a second rock of equal size that now appeared at the right of the first one.

"Guest accommodations," said the Tar. Hopping over the doorsill and into the water, it gestured for me to step onto the path.

I walked to the rock. Its surface was flat and, to my surprise, dry. I sat in a position the Tar had taught me.

"How do we prepare for battle?" it asked, climbing out of the water and onto its rock.

"First we find the quiet place within. Then we reach out to touch the joy that fills the universe."

"Prepare with me," it said.

I nodded, closed my eyes, and tried to attain Katsu Maranda. As the Tar had taught me, I went in my mind to the places and times where I had experienced the greatest happiness, seeking to put myself in joyful harmony with the universe. I saw myself working with the Tar . . . playing with the twins . . . walking through Seldom Seen with my father—

My eyes snapped open. I wasn't very good at this yet. The joyful things and the sorrowful things were too close together, seemed to overlap, so that the brightness and the darkness were mixed together.

I looked to my side. The Tar was sitting on its stone, eyes closed, strange face wreathed in bliss.

I closed my eyes and tried again. I was almost there when the captain's voice called over a speaker, "Tar Gibbons and Deputy Allbright, report to the bridge at once."

The Tar opened its eyes and said simply: "It's time."

Heart pounding, I followed my teacher back to the bridge.

The others had gathered there as well. Each of them solemnly wished the Tar good luck.

The ship's door opened.

The ramp extended.

The Tar stepped out onto it.

I wondered if our plan was crazy, if we shouldn't just try to escape to our dimension while we could. But that would be pointless, since it would leave Smorkus Flinders free to tear a permanent hole between the dimensions.

He had to be stopped here.

He had to be stopped now.

And Tar Gibbons had to do it.

I found myself saying a little prayer as the Tar left the ship. I didn't think I could stand it if anything happened to my new teacher.

That was the first time I realized that I had come to love the Tar.

Elspeth came and stood next to me. We watched

through the ship's view screen as the Tar positioned its lemon-shaped body in front of the ship. Turning to face us, the four-legged alien made a sign that it was ready.

Phil threw a switch.

Nothing happened.

Grakker cursed. "What's the matter?" he snapped. "Why isn't the Tar growing?"

"The enlarging ray isn't focusing properly," replied Phil. "There must be something wrong with the lens."

"Why didn't—never mind. What has to be done to fix it?"

"Fastest way would be to replace the lens. It's a fairly simple operation."

Suddenly Plink shot out from under Phil's leaves and disappeared through the door. Seconds later he came scooting back into the cabin, carrying a clear circle.

Grakker hesitated for less than a second, then said, "Deputy Allbright, take this out and install it."

I felt my stomach tighten with fear.

"Why are you sending him?" cried Elspeth. "He's just a kid! He could get killed out there!"

"Silence!" snapped Grakker.

As captain, he didn't need to explain the reasons for his decision. Besides, I already understood them. With Snout missing and the Tar outside, the crew was down to four: Phil, Grakker, Madame Pong . . . and me. Phil was needed inside to operate the enlarging ray as soon as it was fixed. Madame Pong and Grakker were both more important to the overall success of the mission than I was. And on top of all that, I had already done one repair job on the enlarging/shrinking rays and had some familiarity with the device.

"Come here, Rod," said Phil. Tendrils snaking rapidly over the control panel, he called up a diagram on a small view screen. "Do you see what you need to do?"

I nodded. "Simple," I said. *As long as I live through it,* I added in my head.

Plink handed me the lens. The ship's door opened. They didn't extend the ramp; it wasn't necessary for this operation.

Elspeth grabbed the chibling and held it back while I climbed onto the ledge that circled the ship. Quickly I began to make my way up the side. My work with the Tar had paid off; I moved with a kind of strength and agility I had never had before, making it to the top in a matter of seconds.

I had almost finished the repair when Smorkus Flinders walked through one of the walls.

I stood for a moment, frozen with horror, then dropped to the top of the ship, praying that the monster wouldn't see me.

Was that wise and cautious, or an act of sheer cowardice? I have asked myself that question a thousand times since that horrifying moment.

All I know is that my delay meant that the enlarging ray was not ready.

Probably there would not have been time to enlarge Tar Gibbons to Smorkus Flinders's size before the monster struck anyway. That doesn't make any difference. The images I still carry in my mind are of Smorkus Flinders roaring with rage; Smorkus Flinders storming across the room; Smorkus Flinders bending down in front of the tiny Tar, and with one enormous finger flicking him so hard that his four-legged body flies across the room.

The Tar smashed into a wall. His limp body slid to the floor.

Smorkus Flinders glanced at the ship, then turned to look for the fallen Tar. I realized then another reason why Grakker had kept everyone else inside the ship. *The monster didn't know we were there!* He thought the Tar had come alone.

But now what?

Grakker's words to the Tar echoed in my mind. *"Both law and custom dictate that if you should fall, your apprentice must take up the battle."*

Ridiculous. I couldn't possibly fight Smorkus Flinders. I didn't have the training. I hadn't worked long enough or hard enough.

Cold fear shivered through me as a voice in my head whispered, *"If not you, then who?"*

Smorkus Flinders planned to destroy my home, my solar system, my universe.

Who else was there to stop him?

Moving as silently as I could, I dropped the lens into place.

Smorkus Flinders was still searching for the Tar's body.

I slid off the front of the ship, raced to the place where the Tar had stood, and waved my arms.

Nothing happened.

I had to get their attention, and fast; I had to grow before the monster saw that I was there.

Suddenly I remembered trying to talk to Smorkus Flinders back in Seldom Seen, remembered how he hadn't been able to hear me until he had jammed me into his ear.

"The ray is fixed!" I screamed. "Turn it on! *Turn it on!*"

A beam of orange light shot from the top of the *Ferkel*.

I stood there, trying to put myself in joyful harmony with the universe.

It would have been easier if Smorkus Flinders hadn't found the Tar at precisely that moment. Picking up my teacher's tiny body, he turned back toward the table just in time to see me start to grow.

CHAPTER
20

Battle of the Titans

I HAD EXPERIENCED THE ENLARGING RAY DURING OUR first adventure, when the aliens returned me from two inches to my regular size. I had blacked out briefly when that happened. This time I didn't lose consciousness, even though being turned into a giant was much, much worse than simply returning to my natural size.

I suspect the only reason I managed to stay conscious was that my work with Tar Gibbons had made me so much more fit than the first time I had been enlarged.

Even so, the stretching made me weak and woozy. So I was in no condition to respond when Smorkus Flinders tossed the Tar's body onto the table and smacked me sideways, out of reach of the enlarging ray.

By the time I hit the floor, I was three times my normal height, but less than a midget compared to Smorkus Flinders. He lifted his foot to stomp on me. He probably would have driven me right through the floor, which was in the process of turning into a wall, if the *Ferkel* had not shot up from the table to hover over me, bathing me in the enlarging ray again.

Snarling, Smorkus Flinders turned to swat at the ship. The *Ferkel* darted away.

I had grown another ten feet.

The monster dithered for a moment, uncertain whether he should attack me or the *Ferkel*. The Tar had trained *me* not to dither. Stretching sideways, I thrust my feet between Smorkus Flinders's legs, twisted, and sent him tumbling.

He struck the floor like an avalanche.

That settled the question for him. Roaring in anger, he launched himself at me.

I had enough wit to roll out of the way.

The *Ferkel* soared overhead again and gave me another shot of the enlarging ray.

Smorkus Flinders should have attacked me while I was growing, since I was too woozy then to defend myself. Instead, he threw himself back at the *Ferkel*—reasoning, I assume, that he had to stop it before it actually made me bigger than he was.

The *Ferkel* weaved and dipped. Smorkus Flinders lunged back and forth, trying to catch it so he could smash it.

I climbed to my feet. I was taller than a tele-

phone pole now—huge, but still not even half the monster's height.

A few weeks earlier I would have thought there was no chance at all of overcoming such a difference in size. But the Tar had taught me differently. Gathering my strength, I prepared to launch myself at Smorkus Flinders.

Suddenly the monster turned away from the ship. I braced myself, thinking that he was going to come after me. But to my horror and astonishment, he instead dashed to the table. Snatching up the Tar's body he roared, "Stop where you are! Stop, or I squash!"

Then he curled his fingers over our fallen comrade, ready to make good on his threat.

The *Ferkel* came to a halt, hovering in the air like someone treading water.

Smorkus Flinders held his hand out flat, then placed his other hand above it. "On your knees, Earth boy!" he said to me. "On your knees or I clap."

I fell to my knees, my heart pounding with fear for the Tar.

"To the floor!" he roared, pointing at the *Ferkel*.

I held my breath, waiting to see what Grakker would do.

The *Ferkel* settled gently to the floor.

Smorkus Flinders walked to it and placed one

foot on top of it. I wondered if he was planning to stomp on it.

Grinning at me, he curled his fingers around the Tar's body once again. "Maybe I'll squash him anyway," he said.

"I don't think so!" cried a tiny voice. To my astonishment, a beautiful winged creature darted out of Smorkus Flinders's hand. It was Galuspa! He must have shaped himself to look like the wounded Tar and replaced him during the first part of my fight with Smorkus Flinders.

I glanced at the table. The real Tar's body was nowhere in sight. Hoping that the other shape-shifters had somehow hidden him, I launched myself at Smorkus Flinders, caught him in midsection, and drove him to his knees.

The *Ferkel* shot into the air.

Suddenly I realized that even though he was enormous, Smorkus Flinders was not a good fighter. In a way, it made sense. Spar Kellis had told us that they judged beings on the basis of their size here. Since Smorkus Flinders was the biggest thing on the planet, odds were he had never had to fight much; the other monsters had deferred to him simply because of his size.

Though I had struck at the monster out of rage over what he had been willing to do to Tar Gibbons—and with the faint hope that I might buy enough time for the *Ferkel* to escape—I was now taken by the totally weird idea that I might actually be able to beat him!

That thought lasted until he hit me. Smorkus Flinders's lack of skill was more than made up for by the fact that he was still twice my size. Groaning with pain, I stumbled backward and fell to the floor again. My stomach hurt so much that I might have given up then and there, if I hadn't already learned to deal with that kind of pain from getting beat up by Billy Becker all through sixth grade.

Besides, the Tar had been teaching me how to get past pain, how to put it out of my mind until later. I took a deep breath and staggered to my feet, still woozy from the growing ray. It didn't help that the *Ferkel* chose that moment to give me still another shot of it—though the fact that I put on an additional twenty feet, bringing me up to chest height with Smorkus Flinders, spooked my opponent so much that it was almost worth it.

Crouching, I began to circle slowly to the left. Smorkus Flinders pivoted in place, bracing himself for my attack. Perfect; I *wanted* him to think I was getting ready to attack. The truth was, I was just stalling for time, hoping the wooziness would pass.

Finally the monster roared with frustration and threw himself at me.

I ducked, bent forward, and sent him flying over my back.

When he crashed to the floor, I turned and flung myself on top of him.

Just as quickly he flung me off.

I lay still, facedown. Smorkus Flinders threw himself on top of me, pinning me to the floor. He grunted with satisfaction, thinking that he had won, until he realized that he still had to do something with me. He tried to roll me over. I didn't make it easy. I was ignoring him, ignoring the fight, trying to touch the deeper streams of joy, to find the greater strength.

I located it in a memory of bopping the twins good-night with their teddy bears. Suddenly I had the Katsu Maranda. I hadn't even noticed that Smorkus Flinders had been pounding my back. Shouting the Tar's battle cry of "Hee-yah! Frizzim Spezzack!" I rolled over and trapped the monster beneath me, pinning his shoulders to the floor.

To my astonishment, he began to cry.

"Don't hurt me," he whimpered.

I should have known better. I shouldn't have been so naive. But when someone with the size and face of Smorkus Flinders starts to cry, it's hard not to feel sorry for him. And at the moment I had no desire to hurt him, only to stop him.

That moment of foolish weakness on my part was all it took. With a laugh Smorkus Flinders threw me off. At once he was on his feet. The joy left my heart, replaced by a black rage at letting myself be tricked. At once my strength faded. I had lost the Katsu Maranda, and the wooziness that came with being enlarged overwhelmed me again. Seconds later I was flat on my back, Smorkus Flinders's hands around my throat, his hideous face pressed close to mine.

His breath alone was enough to kill a person.

I heard a sound, a hiss and a sizzle, and realized that the *Ferkle* was shooting bolts of energy at him.

I could smell burning flesh. If it caused him any pain, Smorkus Flinders ignored it. He continued to tighten his grip on my neck, staring into my eyes, laughing.

The world swam back before me as I began to lose consciousness. I was almost out when I heard Snout's voice whisper in my head: *Rod, don't give up!*

Snout? I thought in astonishment. *Is that you?*

I may have been unconscious at that point; I'm not certain. I *am* certain that it truly was our missing friend—and not just because his next words to me were, *Yes, Rod, it really is me.* The certainty came from something deeper, having to do, I now understand, with the link he had established between us back when he did the training transfer.

Where are you? I thought.

You have to understand that this was happening in milliseconds, far faster than I can explain it.

I can't tell you. But I have to give you a message.

What is it?

Smorkus Flinders can tell you something about your father. He knows something, but I'm not sure what. I have to . . . No, don't! Rod, the Ferkada. Tell Grakker that the Ferkada has me!

And then he was gone.

My eyes flew open. I lifted my hands and thrust them between Smorkus Flinders's arms, arms that were huge and knotted with muscles. Though those muscles were bulging with the effort of choking the life out of me, they were like butter in the face of my righteous indignation.

With one sharp move I snapped my hands apart, breaking his grip on my throat. In another move I had rolled over and was on top of him.

I shall never forget the look of terror on Smorkus Flinders's face as I began to smash his head against the floor, screaming, *"Where is my father? What did you do with my father?"*

"BKR!" he cried. "You'll have to ask BKR! He's the only one who knows!"

It was about then that I blacked out.

CHAPTER
21

The Secret

I WAS IN THE SHIP WHEN I WOKE.

"What happened?" I asked, trying to sit up. "Where's the Tar?"

"Shhhh," said Madame Pong. "Try and rest for now."

Looking up, I saw a blue light above me, and realized that I was on one of the *Ferkel*'s healing tables. The chibling was lying at my feet, making its happy sound.

On a table not far away, I saw my teacher.

"Is the Tar all right?" I asked, forcing the words past the lump in my throat.

Madame Pong smiled. "Given a little more time on the table your teacher will be as good as new—as will you, Rod. But you *do* need time. Close your eyes now and rest."

"But I have to tell you what happened!" I said. "I have to tell you . . ."

Only I couldn't tell her anything, because sleep had claimed me again. It might have been a side effect of the healing table. It might have been the aftermath of being enlarged. It might have been pure exhaustion.

Whatever it was, I couldn't resist it.

The next time I woke, Elspeth was sitting beside me.

"You were so cool, Rod," she said, her eyes wide. "I can't believe you really did that."

"I can't, either," I said, wishing that the room would stop spinning around. I glanced at the table next to me.

The Tar was still there, but its eyes were open now. "You did well, my krevlik," it whispered. "I am proud of you."

I smiled. Somehow my teacher's approval made all the terror and pain seem worthwhile.

"Where were you?" I asked. "I mean after Galuspa took your place?"

"According to Madame Pong, the shapeshifters hid my body underneath them, so that I looked like little more than a lump in the surface of the table."

I grinned. "What about Smorkus Flinders?" I asked. "Where is *he* now?"

"Right here in the ship," said Elspeth. When she saw the look of surprise on my face, she explained further. "You were so big, and holding on to him so tightly, they had to shrink you in order to get you off of him. When they did, Smorkus Flinders shrank, too. Phil told me he thinks that whatever shield Smorkus Flinders had against shrinking was mentally activated and couldn't work once he was unconscious. Anyway, when they finally managed to pry your hands off his neck, they locked him up somewhere. I have no idea what they're going to do with him." She paused, then looked at me seriously. "What got you so upset, Rod? Why were you screaming about your father like that?"

I blinked, trying to remember. Then it hit me. "It was Snout!" I cried. "Snout spoke to me inside my head. He told me that Smorkus Flinders would know something about where my father was."

Elspeth's eyes grew wide. "Do you think that's true?" she whispered.

"I don't think Snout would lie to me," I said. "What I can't understand is how he was able to speak to me at all! He wouldn't tell me where he was. Then . . ." I could feel myself grow pale as I remembered the rest of it. "Then we were cut off somehow. He sounded upset. He said to tell Grakker that the Ferkada had him."

The Tar raised its head and said urgently, "We must tell the captain about this at once. Elspeth, please go get Grakker."

174

To my astonishment, Elspeth agreed without a fuss. When she came back, she had with her not only Grakker, but Madame Pong, Phil, Galuspa, and the Ting Wongovia.

I repeated my story.

Grakker began to tremble. The look on his face was impossible for me to interpret.

"What's the Ferkada?" I asked.

"I do not know," said Madame Pong. Her voice sounded troubled. She turned to the Ting Wongovia. "Do you?"

The Ting Wongovia looked away. When he turned back, his eyes were filled with a strange mixture of emotions—fear and longing, hope and horror, all mingled in one.

"The Ferkada is only whispered of among my people," he said. "Some call it evil. Some say it was a thing of great beauty that was misunderstood. More than that is not said, nor do I think it is known, unless by the greatest masters. That my egg-brother is in the grip of the Ferkada is a thing of wonder. But I do not know what it means."

"Where is this Ferkada?" growled Grakker.

The Ting Wongovia shook his head. "I have told you all that I know. To find out more, you will have to visit the Mentat. And they do not like visitors."

"What about my father?" I asked. "When BKR

said that he knew where Dad was, we all thought he was lying just to be cruel. Now Smorkus Flinders says the same thing—that BKR knows. What's going on here?"

Madame Pong looked at Grakker. He hesitated, then nodded.

"Rod," she said. "We have not been completely honest with you."

I didn't like the sound of that. "Go on," I said uneasily.

Madame Pong's cheeks turned a deep orange. She was blushing—an astonishing thing for a diplomat. "It was not entirely an accident that we landed in your room that day," she said.

My throat felt dry. "Are you going to tell me why not?" I asked after a moment.

She closed her eyes. "We were looking for your father."

I could feel my stomach getting tighter, my heart beating faster.

"Why?" I whispered.

"Because he was missing, obviously," said Grakker.

"Lots of people on Earth go missing," I said. "Don't tell me that you go looking for all of them."

"Of course not," said Madame Pong.

"Then why . . . ?" I stopped, my throat dry. "Why were you looking for *him?*"

"I think you know," said Madame Pong.

I closed my eyes. I felt like a hand was pressing down on me, squeezing the air out of my lungs. Silence hung heavy in the air. Finally I opened my eyes again.

"He's one of you, isn't he?" I asked.

"One of the greatest," said Madame Pong gently.

Elspeth looked at me in astonishment. "Oh, my god." She gasped. "Rod—*you're an alien!*"

EPILOGUE

Some things take a while to get used to. Finding out that you're an alien—well, half-alien—when you've spent your entire life thinking you're an Earthling is one of them.

What's weird is, I still don't know if my mother knows or not. I mean about my father. Naturally, if she knows about him, then she knows about *me*.

What she doesn't know yet is that I have to go looking for Dad.

Frankly, I'm not looking forward to telling her. But I don't really have a choice. My father is out there, somewhere, and I have to go find him.

Elspeth insists that she's going to come along, too, but I don't think the aliens are going to go along with that.

The aliens. I have to stop thinking of them that way. The crew of the *Ferkel*, I should say. Grakker, Madame Pong, Tar Gibbons, Phillogenous esk Piemondum—and me, Rod Allbright.

And Snout, if we can ever find him.

Boy, have we got a lot to do.

But at least Earth, and the galaxy, in fact our whole dimension, are safe from the Reality Quakes. At least I don't have to worry about Mom and the twins turning into monsters. (Well, sometimes the twins are little monsters. And now that I think of it, they must be half alien. But you know what I mean.)

I'm not sure what we're going to do with Smorkus Flinders yet. We may turn him over to Spar Kellis and the other monsters. We may take him along with us, on the theory that he knows more about BKR's plans than we have been able to find out so far.

Tomorrow we say good-bye to Galuspa and the others. I still can't get over what a good guy Spar Kellis turned out to be. Well, except for one thing. He wanted a reward for helping us.

"What, exactly, do you want?" asked Grakker suspiciously.

Looking a little embarrassed, the big blue monster wiped a line of drool from his chin and said, "Those."

He was pointing at my sneakers.

"Are you kidding?" I asked.

Spar Kellis shook his head. "I have very tender feet. Those look comfortable."

I looked at Madame Pong. She nodded. I took off my sneakers, and we used the *Ferkel*'s enlarging beam to blow them up to fit Spar Kellis.

The aliens gave me a good pair of boots to replace them.

My mother probably won't be amused. After all, she did ask me not to wear my new sneakers when I went out to the field that day.

On the other hand, when I tell her everything else that I have to tell her, the fact that I left my sneakers in Dimension X will probably be the least of her worries.

About the Author and Illustrator

BRUCE COVILLE was born in Syracuse, New York. He grew up in a rural area, around the corner from his grandfather's dairy farm. Halloween was his favorite holiday, his school's official colors were orange and black, and as a teenager he made extra money by digging graves—all of which probably helps explain why he writes the kind of books he does. He has written nearly four dozen books for children, including *My Teacher Is an Alien, Goblins in the Castle, Aliens Ate My Homework* (the first title in the *Rod Allbright Alien Adventures* series), *The Dragonslayers,* and the *Space Brat* books.

KATHERINE COVILLE is a self-taught artist who is known for her ability to combine finely detailed drawings with a deliciously wacky sense of humor. She is also a toymaker, specializing in creatures hitherto unseen on this planet. She likes miniatures, and once made a dollhouse inside an acorn. Her other collaborations with Bruce Coville include *The Monster's Ring, The Foolish Giant, Sarah's Unicorn, Goblins in the Castle, Aliens Ate My Homework, The Dragonslayers,* and the *Space Brat* books.

The Covilles live in a big, old house along with an assortment of odd children, a dog named Booger, and two cats named Spike and Thunder.